"Is that a wate

"It is," Gabe answer

"Up on blocks?"

"The base is called an underdresser. There wasn't enough space for the bed and a bureau, so I have drawers in the base of the bed," he explained, amused at her curiosity.

"And you need a ladder to get into bed." Gracie couldn't resist going over to the bed and pushing down on the black quilt that covered the mattress.

"Have you ever slept on a waterbed?"

Was that a proposition? No, it just sounded as if he were asking a simple question. "Never."

"You don't know what you're missing. Lie down on it and see what it's like."

Then at her hesitation, he leaned a shoulder against the far wall and crossed his arms over his chest. "I promise I'll stay all the way over here...."

Dear Reader,

Welcome to Silhouette **Special Edition** . . . welcome to romance. Each month, Silhouette **Special Edition** publishes six novels with you in mind—stories of love and life, tales that you can identify with—romance with that little "something special" added in.

July is a wonderful month—full of sizzling stories packed with emotion. Don't miss Debbie Macomber's warm and witty *Bride on the Loose*—the concluding tale of her series, THOSE MANNING MEN. And *Heartbreak Hank* is also in store for you—Myrna Temte's third COWBOY COUNTRY tale. Starting this month, as well, is Linda Lael Miller's new duo BEYOND THE THRESHOLD. The initial book is entitled *There and Now*.

Rounding out this month are more stories by some of your favorite authors: Bevlyn Marshall, Victoria Pade and Laurie Paige.

In each Silhouette **Special Edition** novel, we're dedicated to bringing you the romances that you dream about— stories that will delight as well as bring a tear to the eye. For me, good romance novels have always contained an element of hope, of optimism that life can be, and often is, very beautiful. I find a great deal of inspiration in that thought.

Why do you read romances? I'd really like to hear your opinions on the books that we publish and on the romance genre in general. Please write to me c/o Silhouette Books, 300 East 42nd Street, 6th floor, New York, NY 10017.

I hope that you enjoy this book and all of the stories to come. Looking forward to hearing from you!

Sincerely,

Tara Gavin
Senior Editor
Silhouette Books

VICTORIA PADE
Amazing Gracie

Silhouette Special Edition
Published by Silhouette Books New York
America's Publisher of Contemporary Romance

SILHOUETTE BOOKS
300 East 42nd St., New York, N.Y. 10017

AMAZING GRACIE

Copyright © 1992 by Victoria Pade

ISBN: 0-373-09752-2

First Silhouette Books printing July 1992

Books by Victoria Pade

VICTORIA PADE,

bestselling author of both historical and contemporary romance fiction, is the mother of two energetic daughters, Cori and Erin. Although she enjoys her chosen career as a novelist, she occasionally laments that she has never traveled farther from her Colorado home than Disneyland, instead spending all her spare time plugging away at her computer. She takes breaks from writing by indulging in her favorite hobby—eating chocolate.

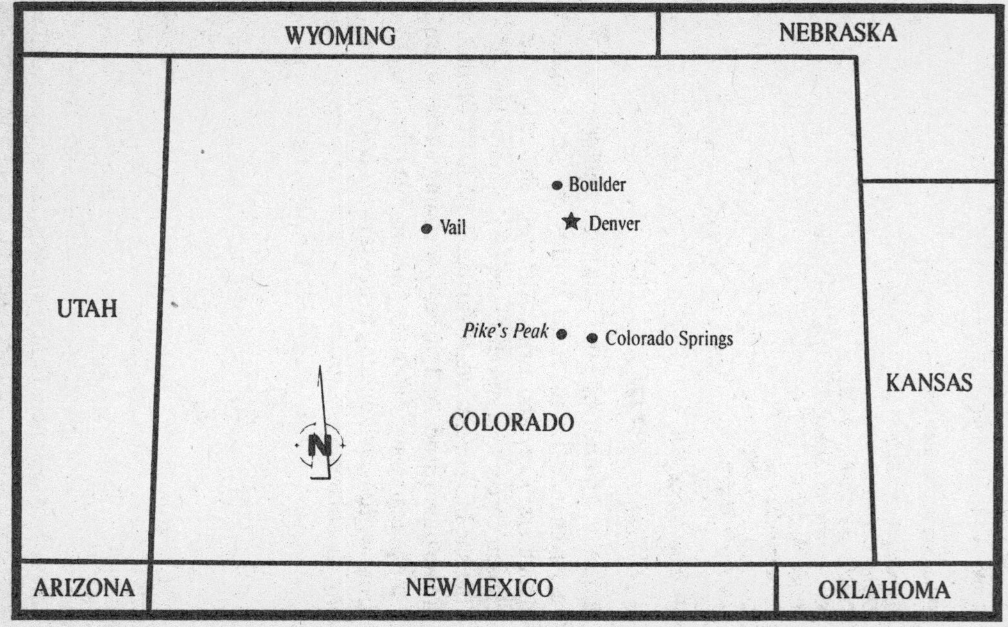

WYOMING
NEBRASKA
Boulder
Vail
Denver
UTAH
Pike's Peak
Colorado Springs
KANSAS
COLORADO
N
ARIZONA
NEW MEXICO
OKLAHOMA

Chapter One

The years had not been kind to the place, Gracie Canon thought as she climbed down from her cousin's van in front of the house she'd inherited from her great-aunt Adeline. A ninety-year-old Victorian gingerbread with a third-floor attic, the house stood out among the much more contemporary structures that comprised the up-scale section of the Long Gate area just outside metropolitan Denver.

Even in the meager light of a streetlamp and the glow of a full moon in the inky night sky, Gracie could tell the surrounding wrought-iron fence was wobbly between brick supporting members that stood like stoic sentries. The lawn needed weeding, the house's exterior paint was peeling, some of the corner lattices were missing and the gutters were chipped. Gracie knew that her aunt Adeline had been too busy with her charities, causes and all of the new interests that were forever capturing her attention to notice such minor things as upkeep.

"Remember, you're always welcome to stay with me," Gracie's cousin Wilhamena said.

"Thanks, anyway." Gracie pulled her carry-on case out from in front of the van seat and pushed the door closed, quietly enough so as not to wake the neighbors at this late hour. But she might as well have slammed it, because opening the iron gate made it creak a loud announcement.

"Geez," Willy muttered under her breath from just behind Gracie.

Gracie bent over to pick up a flyer from the redbrick walk that led to the porch that Adeline called the veranda, sweeping one side of her chin-length, strawberry-blond hair behind her ear when she stood back up.

With Willy close on her heels, she climbed the steps to the porch, rummaging in her big, baggy purse for the keys. Once she found them she opened the screen, discovering that it was off its top hinge and hung forward when not braced within the jamb.

"Hang on to this, will you?" she asked of Willy, who held the screen while Gracie used her key in the ancient lock on the front door. Then she turned the ball-shaped knob and pushed.

The door didn't budge.

After three more unsuccessful shoves Gracie put her shoulder and hip to the oak that framed an oval of beveled glass and rammed the thing until it finally gave way, setting off an answering thud that sounded as if it came from the furnace, in spite of the fact that it was late July and the old relic certainly wasn't in use.

"Too bad. I was hoping we wouldn't be able to get the door open," Willy said under her breath.

Two steps into the entranceway made the peg-and-groove floor squeak. Gracie felt for the light switch, flipping it up once she'd found it. The overhead brass fixture flickered for a moment before glowing—much like a flame trying to catch hold of a candlewick in the wind.

Willy came in after her. She replaced the screen securely in the jamb and closed the door.

The place was clean; Adeline was a stickler for tidiness and hadn't been gone long enough for much dust to gather, even on the banister of the steep staircase directly in front of them. But the air was hot and thick from the house being closed up.

Gracie went into the living room to her left, opening a window on the side wall where the glass rattled and the frame protested with a groan. Paying it no attention, she turned into the center of the room and took a look around.

She raised her green eyes to the tin ceiling, then dropped them downward to the Persian rug that covered all but the perimeters of the floor. She glanced next into the corner at the carved oak fireplace before letting her gaze drift into the center of the room at the Turkish chair and sofa in dark maroon tufted velvet, and the genuine Tiffany lamps with rose-colored glass forming tulips. There was a black wicker rocking chair with a big peacock back angled in from a second corner, and beside it was a marble-topped table with a wood-and-wire bird cage on top of it. The third and last corner held only a big globe in a mahogany stand.

"Yuk," Willy said as she looked in from the hallway. "I've never cared for this place."

Gracie smiled. "And I just love it."

"You have to be kidding," Willy said as they headed back outside for the rest of Gracie's bags.

The bright, rainbow-colored stripes painted on the side of the vehicle separated as Willy slid open the door. "I can't believe you're actually happy to move into Adeline's house and take over every odd bit of junk she's collected in her eighty-two years."

"I don't know why that should surprise you, Willy. Remember, I restore furniture like this for a living. To me this whole place has charm and character."

"And no shower."

"I only take baths."

"But everything is so *old*." Willy drew the word out into a complaint as she hoisted a suitcase and handed it to Gracie.

"Everything is seasoned," Gracie corrected, heading back into the house. "I've renovated pieces for museums that aren't as high a quality as what Adeline left me. Do you know what kind of workmanship went into hand carving that Bible stand next to the fireplace? Do you know how old that family Bible is? Or how many pieces of our history are recorded in it? How many births and deaths led in one way or another to you and I being here right at this moment?"

Willy rolled her eyes. "Do you know how many times I've heard these lectures? For as long as I can remember. From you it's the artistry in every ancient relic you come across and from your brother it's the value in it. To me, a bunch of somebody's old used junk is just a bunch of somebody's old used junk."

"Are you sure we're related?" Gracie asked, laughing at her cousin.

"It's your mother's fault, you know," Willy countered. "She went and married your father and brought home all her rummage-sale finds for him to refinish. My father left his carpentry skills at the shop on the week-ends but yours had to go home and remake somebody's crummy broken-apart something that they didn't want cluttering up their basement anymore.''

Gracie led the way back outside for the last of her luggage, smiling as her cousin continued her tirade from behind.

"And while I'm at this, how come Dean turned into the antique dealer like your mother and you turned into the renovator like your father?''

"Natural selection, I guess. Dean was too much of a klutz to handle the scroll saw without cutting his fingers off.''

With all the baggage out, Willy slid the van door closed. "Well, all I can say is I'm glad you're going to live here now so you and your brother can marvel over this stuff to each other. When Burt got transferred to Connecticut it was bad enough that Dean called you long-distance half the time and me the other half to glory in all of his big finds. But in these past six months since you've been in Australia he's driven me nuts. I swear he calls me every time he makes a deal for a cup that's more than ten years old.''

"I'm glad to be back, too,'' Gracie said over her shoulder as she set a suitcase on the entry floor and closed the front door. When she turned to Willy again, her cousin's dark eyes were as round as marbles and she looked as if she wanted to bite off her tongue.

"What's the matter?'' Gracie asked.

"Should I not have mentioned Burt?''

Gracie made a face and shook her head. "Burt died in a car accident, Willy, he didn't run off with the next-door neighbor's wife.''

"I know, but it's only been six months,'' Willy whispered.

"It's okay," Gracie whispered back.

"But are you okay? I mean, you were pretty messed up."

"Nobody loses someone they love and doesn't get pretty messed up, Wil. But I'm all right now. Taking the job renovating the antiques for the archives in Australia was just what I needed—time away from everything to grieve and get my head straight again. Now I'm ready to reenter the land of the living." Gracie held her arms straight out from her sides and winked. "I'm baa-aack."

Willy sniffed a little and cleared her throat, so when she went on her voice was loud and firm once again. "Well, all I can say is I'm glad that when our ditsy great-aunt decided to spend the rest of her life sequestered in a Tibetan monastery, she left me her stock portfolio instead of this place. She was right—you are the only one of us kids who wouldn't race to sell or trash this house and all her old junk along with it."

Gracie smiled, appreciating the evidence of her cousin's sympathies even if Willy wasn't comfortable showing them for too long. "And all I can say is that I'm glad she left you her stock portfolio, too, and left me this house and all her old junk. She couldn't have chosen a better time, since I wanted to come back to Colorado and all my family when the job in Australia was finished, anyway. Adeline left me a place to come home to."

The grandfather clock chimed eleven and they both glanced at it in the alcove off the foot of the steps where it had been housed for as long as either of them could remember.

"I didn't realize it was so late," Gracie said as she brought a suitcase from the living room, picked up the one she'd set in the entryway and climbed the stairs.

"That traffic jam at the airport is what did it." Willy grabbed all she could carry and followed.

Gracie stopped for a moment once she'd reached the doorway of the master bedroom on the second floor. It was large but most of the space was taken up by an enormous bed that, although it was only a double width, had an eight-foot-high headboard and a three-foot-high footboard, both in solid mahogany. Gracie had always loved that bed. And now it was hers.

"You don't have to stick around if you'd rather head home," she said to Willy then, stepping into the room. "I'm just going to make the bed and get in it."

Willy set down the suitcases she'd carried up. "I'll help you and then take off."

"Open the windows while I get some sheets, why don't you, then?" Gracie said as she went into the hallway to the linen closet.

"Better see if you can find the pillow Adeline kept for guests after she gave up sleeping on one herself," Willy called to her.

The sheets were stacked on the uppermost shelf. At barely five feet three inches Gracie couldn't reach them, let alone see past them for a pillow. She had to drag a chair from the desk in the end bedroom.

"Come here and hold these sheets so I can look behind them, will you?"

Willy appeared at her side and took the perfectly folded stack of crisp, white linens.

Standing on her toes, Gracie ducked inside the closet, her voice a muffled echo as she reached as far back as she could into the four-foot depth. "I found it, but something's coming out with it," she called as she dragged the pillow forward.

Backing out of the closet, Gracie clasped the pillow between her knees and took down an old flowered hatbox. "Oh, look, it's Adeline's *treasure chest,*" she said with a laugh.

"I used to love getting into that thing," Willy admitted.

"Me, too." Gracie propped it against one hip, took all but two sheets from Willy and replaced them on the shelf while Willy pulled the pillow from between Gracie's knees and went back into the bedroom.

Gracie hopped off the chair and followed her, hatbox in hand. She set it on the bare feather mattress and lifted the lid. "These were my favorites for dress-up," she said, clipping on a pair of big silver daisy-shaped earrings, one of them missing the purple stone out of the center. "And the beads!" She draped all ten strands around her neck.

"I liked the fingerless gloves," Willy said as she put them on. "And the black knitted skullcap from the roaring twenties. I was so crazy about it I begged and begged Adeline to let me take it home so I could wear it to school."

Gracie wrinkled her nose. "I never liked the hat. *I* had to have the feathers in my hair." Gracie poked the bedraggled plumes behind her ear.

"And sunglasses—who cares if the lenses are a little cracked?" Willy put them on.

"And bracelets up to my elbow." Gracie slipped a dozen up her arm with dramatic flair.

"And the aviator's scarf. Even if it was moth-eaten, I always had to wear the scarf and carry the beaded evening purse—missing beads and all—tucked under my arm just the way Adeline did when she went downtown." Willy wrapped the scarf twice around her throat, tossed the ends over her shoulders and jammed the purse into her armpit as they both laughed like the kids they'd been the last time they'd explored their great-aunt's hatbox treasure chest.

"What's this?" Gracie asked.

Willy's removal of the aviator's scarf had left an assortment of other odds and ends—more earrings, several brooches, some handkerchiefs and a photograph.

"Oh, look, it's a picture of Adeline and Eli Duran—it must have fallen out of an album and just been tossed in here."

Willy craned her neck to see over Gracie's shoulder. "Where do you suppose they were? They look so young."

Gracie turned the photo over and read, " 'Trip to New Mexico with Eli, 1960.' " Then she flipped it back to the picture side. "Do you believe the expression on Adeline's face? I think she wanted to jump his bones."

"You know she did. She always had the hots for Eli Duran."

"True." Gracie laughed. "I must have heard her say a million times that if he hadn't been such a womanizer he was the only man in the world she would have considered marrying—even if he was fifteen years younger than her."

"And instead they've just been friends for decades, unless, of course, our old aunt was ahead of her time in the free-love department."

"Mmm, I don't think so. Adeline was pretty old-fashioned when it came to romance," Gracie said. "Remember the day when we were fifteen that she caught us kissing those two brothers from down the street? Now *that* was a lecture. I'm pretty sure she and Eli were just good friends."

"Good enough friends for her to leave him her Rolls-Royce," Willy pointed out.

The doorbell rang just then, a tired-sounding, off-key chime. Exchanging a look with Willy that said, "Who could that be at this hour?" Gracie did a fast skip down the stairs.

She could see through the center of the beveled-glass oval in the door. There was a man standing on the other side, but in the dark she couldn't tell much more than that, so she flipped on the porch light.

He was tall and his athlete's body was dressed in a pair of snug jeans and a black, crewneck T-shirt that echoed the color of his dark hair. His hands were jammed into his back pockets and a slight frown pulled his thick, dark eyebrows, shadowing his eyes and giving him what Adeline would have called "rebel good looks."

But Gracie didn't recognize him and she wondered if he was the kind of guy a woman should open her door to at eleven-thirty at night. Then again, Long Gate was a nice area, Adeline knew all her neighbors and they all knew her, so this was probably one of them making sure whoever was in the vacant house had a right to be.

The man raised one hand at her then and gave a negligent little wave that said he could see her, and Gracie felt obliged to open the door.

"Hi," he said in a deep voice that sounded as if it had to pass a long way through a gravelly throat to get out. He poked a thumb over his shoulder without taking his eyes off her. "I'm Gabe Duran. I live in the house across the street."

Relief washed over Gracie and she smiled. "You're Eli Duran's son. Adeline left me a note about you," she said, thinking that for some reason she hadn't expected the son of Adeline's friend to be so near her own thirty-four years. "My cousin and I were just talking about your father. I'm Gracie Canon—Adeline's niece."

She opened the screen, keeping hold of it so it wouldn't fall and break the hinge that still attached it to the jamb. "Come on in. Sorry about the door but—"

"I know. I've been trying to get Adeline to hire my handyman to do some repairs around here, but the old girl had more things going on than ten people and she never got around to it."

He slipped through the narrow doorway in front of Gracie, close enough for her to catch a whiff of a very pleasant, woodsy-smelling after-shave.

She replaced the screen and closed the door, turning to look at Gabe Duran in the full glow of the entryway light.

Ruggedly good-looking was what she'd call him, Gracie thought. He had a strong jaw; lips that weren't too full or too wide, but just right; a perfect, straight nose; and only the beginning hint of lines dipping from the sides of his nostrils to bracket the corners of his mouth. There were three more faint creases running horizontally across his forehead and a couple fanning out from the corners of his eyes—eyes that were a pretty incredible shade of blue that she couldn't quite put a name to.

And what about that shiny chestnut hair? It was cut short on the sides, longer on top, and she wondered if it always had that slightly mussed, careless look or if the late hour had something to do with it. She'd bet that he'd just swiped a quick hand through it on his way across the street. But whether by accident or design, she had to admit it suited him.

All of a sudden he smiled as if he couldn't control the impulse anymore. One side of his mouth tipped up higher than the other, turning rugged, rebel good looks into rakish ones.

He angled his head, looking at something on the side of hers. "You know, Adeline is by far the most unique woman I've ever met, but even she didn't wear feathers in her hair."

The feathers! And the tacky earrings and the beaded necklaces and the bracelets! Gracie had forgotten them all. She made a scrunched-up face and laughed at herself, rolling her eyes in the direction of the hat plumes stuck behind her ear. "My cousin and I just happened across an old box of things Adeline used to let us play with when we were kids."

"Very nice," he teased.

She held up the photograph she still had in her hand. "We got sidetracked talking about your father when we found this in the box." Gracie handed it to him.

While he glanced at it she slipped the earrings off and took the feathers out of her hair, setting them on the table beside the stairs.

"I guess there wasn't much Adeline didn't get on film even that long ago," he observed. "I've never known anyone who took more pictures or home movies."

"The movies are great, too. Did she ever show you any of them?" Gracie said as she pulled the necklaces over her head, slipped the bracelets off her arm and made a second pile on the table beside the earrings and feathers.

"She was always promising me but she never got around to it, no."

"Oh, well, you'll have to see them sometime."

Gabe placed the photograph with the jewelry she'd just discarded. "I've been keeping an eye on the place and watching for you at the same time. Adeline said you wouldn't know the quirks of the house, so she asked me to walk you through them—not that I came rushing over here to do that now, but the pilot light on the water heater goes out on a regular basis and I didn't think you'd want me to drag my feet about lighting it for you."

As he talked the muscles in his jaw worked, and Gracie was paying more attention to the masculine sight of it than to what he was saying. But she caught up fast. "Adeline said in her note that she'd enlisted you to show me the ropes."

He scratched his eyebrow with his pinkie finger. "Did she tell you anything else in the note?"

Gracie was trying to figure out just what color blue his eyes were. Teal, maybe? No, not quite that green. Then she realized he'd asked her a direct question. "I'm sorry, what did you say?"

"I just asked what else might have been in Adeline's note to you."

"Oh." Gracie briefly wondered why he seemed to think the note should have said something else. "She just scribbled it on one of the lawyer's memo sheets. It said, 'Gracie, Eli's son Gabe lives across the street, he'll show you what you need to know about the house,'" Gracie recited. "That was it."

He nodded as if it were nothing more than he'd expected.

Still, if that were true then why did he ask in the first place? Gracie wondered. Since he seemed disinclined to say anything else, she shrugged. "Well, if memory serves, the water heater and the furnace are both in the laundry room, right?"

"Right."

"Lead the way."

Gabe went down the hall beside the staircase and into the kitchen. The laundry room was through a door in the left wall. It had originally been a mud room, but when gas and electricity were added to the house there had been a need for a place to put the furnace and the appliances they allowed for, so it had become the laundry room.

"If I were you," Gabe said as he took a box of stick matches from on top of the water heater and hunkered down with them, "I'd have the gas connection looked at. Unless you're like your aunt—Adeline said she was crazy about a good, bracing cold bath. I told her she was just plain crazy," he added affectionately.

The man had a great rear end, Gracie thought as she looked down at him. Tight but not so small a woman had to worry that her hips were bigger than his.

Now wait a minute, she said to herself.

Noticing his face, even his body structure, was one thing—that was just part of familiarizing herself with what the man looked like so she'd recognize him next time she saw him. But this was something else again. She hadn't assessed a male posterior since before she'd married Burt. Now was no time to start again.

She recalled that Gabe had said something about the gas connection. "I don't mean to sound dumb, but I've only lived in apartments, except when I was a kid and then my folks took care of things like this." She was babbling and she knew it. Chastising herself for it, she got down to business. "Do you think there's some kind of gas leak? Isn't that dangerous?"

"There isn't a leak or we'd smell it," he told her as he stood, shaking out the match that looked like not much more than a splinter between his strong fingers. "But something keeps the gas from getting to the water heater all the time, and whatever that is should be checked. I told Adeline to have it done, but like I said, she was always too busy."

His eyes were too dark to be lapis but not quite dark enough to be ultramarine. Not that it mattered. "I'll call first chance I get," Gracie assured him, hating that it came out sounding like the words of a good little soldier.

He grinned at her again, and she saw an entreating warmth in it. "There's probably no hurry. As far as I know, Adeline's been having trouble with this pilot light for the last two years and nothing has happened yet. There are plenty of things around this place that are going to have to be looked at, fixed or replaced."

"I guess you'd better give me the information about your handyman, then."

"I'll bring his name and number with me when I come to teach you the rest of the ins and outs. Oh, and while I'm here—" he dug into his right jeans pocket "—I'm sure you want the spare key to the front door. Adeline left it with me in case I needed to get in before you got here."

His eyes were the color of the sky at sunset, she decided. A smoky blue. "Is there—"

"Tallulah? Oh, Tallulah?" Willy called, her tone high-pitched and comical as the sound of her voice drew nearer. "Where'd you get off to, Tallulah? Not fair to leave me to do your bed making for you!"

"Tallulah?" Gabe asked.

"It's a joke. When we'd play dress-up Adeline would call me Tallulah," she explained. Then she raised her voice and aimed it out the door. "We're in the laundry room, Willy."

"We?" Willy said as she appeared in the kitchen. "Oh, hi." She was instantly self-conscious about the sunglasses, gloves, scarf and skullcap she wore, pulling everything off in record speed before she even got to the laundry-room door and holding it behind her back as if she'd been caught stealing.

"This is Gabe Duran—Eli's son," Gracie said.

"I know," Willy answered. "We've met a couple of times since he bought the house across the street." Then, smiling a little feebly, she waved to Gabe. "Hi. I didn't know we had company."

"It's okay, Willy. I told him we were just reliving our childhood," Gracie whispered in an aside.

"And looking like idiots," Willy whispered back.

Gracie fanned the air with her hand. "It doesn't matter. How weird can we seem after Adeline?"

"She has a point," Gabe put in with a laugh.

"So, how come you guys are in the laundry room?" Willy asked.

"Gabe had to light the pilot light on the water heater for me."

"Ahhh." Willy was staring at Gabe as if her eyes were glued to him.

Gracie couldn't help smiling at the sight of her tough-as-nails cousin dumbstruck by an attractive man. She'd never seen anyone have this effect on Willy. Gracie tried to distract Gabe before he noticed. "I was about to ask you if there was anything else I should know right off the bat."

As he thought about it he squatted to check the pilot light and, since he couldn't see what she was doing, Gracie jabbed Willy with her elbow as if knocking a record needle out of a scratch.

Willy rolled her eyes, let her mouth drop open and fanned her face to let Gracie know she thought this guy was too hot to handle.

Then Gabe stood again. "Don't use the toilet in the bathroom down here—it won't flush. The one upstairs must work all right, though, because your aunt didn't say anything about it. I don't think you can get into trouble with anything else for the moment. If you're free I can make some time tomorrow to come over and take you through room by room."

"I'll be here all day. The movers are supposed to bring my furniture out of storage and my car from the garage."

"How about around one, then?" When Gracie agreed, he went out into the kitchen, pointing at the sink there as he passed it as if something had just occurred to him. "There's no garbage disposal, so don't put anything down the drain."

"I'd forgotten. It's a good thing you warned me," Gracie said, trying to ignore the crude pinching gesture Willy was making at Gabe's rear end as they followed him down the hall back to the entranceway. "I really appreciate you watching for me and coming over this late."

"No problem." He opened the front door and turned, cutting short Willy's silent mouthing of "Take me, I'm yours."

"The phone's been removed, so if you want to make a call come over and use mine. And if there's anything else you need, just let me know."

"Thanks, I will."

He held on to the screen as he went out and then set it back in the jamb. "Good night."

"Good night." Gracie closed the door and her cousin collapsed back onto the stairs.

"Isn't he gorgeous? He could light my pilot light anytime.

"You're awful. I couldn't believe you were doing that stuff behind his back. Have you been hanging around construction sites lately, or what?"

"The guy does this to me every time I see him. He's just too cute for me to stand.

"He is pretty cute," Gracie admitted, still watching him through the glass in the door. "But if you ever caught a man doing to you behind your back what you were doing behind his, you'd flatten him."

"I know. It's terrible. I guess I'm just punishing him for never asking me out. Believe me, the couple of times I've met him through Adeline I flirted like crazy, but he never took the hints. Maybe you'll have better luck with him than I did."

"Me?" Gracie said with a full measure of surprise.

Instantly Willy got the same look on her face that she'd had when she'd mentioned Burt. "I'm sorry. I wasn't thinking."

"Would you stop that, Willy? Actually, I guess you're right—I am a single woman again," Gracie said to put her cousin at ease, thinking how strange it seemed to say that. "But if he wasn't interested in you, what makes you think he'd be interested in me?"

"Stranger things have happened," Willy said carefully.

She set the old dress-up things on the table where Gracie had put her portion and went into the living room. When she came back she had her purse.

As Gracie opened the door for her cousin, her gaze strayed to Gabe Duran's back again as he went inside the house across the street.

"Is something wrong out there?" Willy asked.

Gracie realized suddenly that she was frozen in place. She laughed at herself. "I just wanted to make sure he got home safe."

Willy laughed knowingly and gave her a hug. "I'm glad you're back, kid."

"Me, too. Thanks for picking me up at the airport and making my bed. I'll let you know when I get a phone."

"Unless you need me before." Willy went onto the porch and Gracie followed her. "No kidding, Gracie, don't hesitate to call. I know Dean won't be back from that estate sale for a couple of days, and with your folks taking off for Mexico, I'm the next best thing—unless you want to call my parents or the other aunts, uncles or cousins."

The mention of their large extended family caused Gracie to make a face. "You know you're who I'd ask if I needed something. But I'm sure I'll be fine."

Willy nodded over her shoulder at Gabe Duran's house. "I guess you can call your neighbor, too," she said with a wink. "Have you ever seen eyes like those?"

"Never," Gracie admitted with a laugh, glad her cousin had stopped walking on eggshells. "Go home before it gets any later, will you?"

"'Night," Willy called as she got into her van.

Gracie waved, staying to watch her cousin drive off. Then her gaze wandered back to the house across the street.

All the lights were off. Obviously Gabe had gone straight to bed. Maybe he'd been in bed when she and Willy had gotten here and he'd dressed to come over, anyway. Maybe that was why his hair was slightly ruffled.

Suddenly she laughed, shaking her head.

Oh, yes, she was definitely back in the land of the living to be standing on the porch, thinking about her neighbor.

She headed back into the house, locking the door after herself. "It's too soon to be thinking about another man," she told her reflection in the beveled glass. "Much too soon."

Wasn't it?

Chapter Two

Wearing nothing but his boxer shorts the next morning, Gabe opened his front door to get his newspaper. Only after he had stepped a foot outside did he happen to glance up and see Gracie Canon standing at Adeline's picture window.

Cringing internally, he realized there was nothing to do but make the best of it. With the paper strategically positioned, he smiled and waved just before retreating back into the house.

Now that was hardly the impression he wanted to make on his new neighbor—she'd think he was a flasher!

Gracie Canon was still on his mind as he poured his coffee. She was Adeline's favorite great-niece.

"How come you didn't tell me she was so terrific looking?" he asked his absentee friend out loud.

Actually, Gracie reminded him of a young version of Adeline with that very straight, very pale red hair and those sparkling green eyes. She had her aunt's slender nose, too. Only her mouth—with its bare hint of a dip in the center of slightly full lips—was different than Adeline's. And Gracie's cheekbones were higher, too.

"Didn't miss a thing, did I?" he said, surprised at himself. Although when he thought about it he didn't know why it should seem odd that he remembered so many details about Adeline's niece. He'd certainly taken a good enough look last night.

If you were only forty years younger I'd sweep you off your feet. How many times had he told Adeline that since moving across the street from her and becoming friends with her? And now there was Gracie. He'd only been teasing Adeline, but he had to admit to himself that he was definitely feeling an interest in her niece.

He liked a woman who was so unselfconscious that she could be caught dolled up like a kid and only laugh it off. One who seemed at ease with both herself and him. No artifice, no acts. And a body that wasn't bad, either. A little on the short side, maybe, but not so skinny that there was any doubt she was a woman. He liked that, too.

When Adeline had left three weeks ago he'd been sorry to see her go. He'd missed her enthusiastic two-armed waves, and her zany outlook on life. But now, after meeting Gracie, he couldn't help feeling well compensated. And for the first time he was glad that Adeline's old eyesore of a house was right across the street from his and required him to spend some time educating her niece in how to run the place. Getting to know Gracie Canon was a very appealing prospect.

Pouring his second cup of coffee, Gabe called over his shoulder, "Murf! Get up, you twelve-year-old bag of bones."

Nothing happened, so he opened the refrigerator door. "Come on, Murf. No walk today. Just chow."

That did it. The short-haired cocoa-colored Saint Bernard lumbered out of the guest room, his droopy eyes rolled upward to regard Gabe solemnly.

"Don't give me that look." Gabe filled the dog's bowl, gave him fresh water and then went back to the refrigerator for the ingredients to make his special omelet.

He cracked eggs and then dialed the number for The Collector's Exchange, the small shop he owned that specialized in sports cards, gum cards, coins, stamps and comic books.

Ordinarily Gabe ran the store with very little help from anyone. But when he needed a day off he had a retired fireman who came in to handle it for him. And today was definitely a day he needed off.

"Hi, Dave, it's me," he said when his replacement answered the phone. "I just wanted to make sure you got opened up all right."

The older man assured him that he had. There wasn't much Dave needed to be told, so Gabe just said he'd check back later, and they hung up.

He trusted his fill-in implicitly, but, even so, Gabe was always nervous about leaving the store in someone else's hands. Probably because he hadn't been a shop owner for all that long; he'd opened his doors little more than a year ago. Before that he'd been the vice president of a Denver-based oil company. But he'd willingly traded that steady, impressive paycheck for a less hectic, less tension-filled life doing something he loved every day instead of something that made his blood pressure skyrocket.

Not that his life had been less tension filled lately, he thought as he chopped onions and peppers.

The work tensions were gone, but now he was facing the bigger stress of worrying that he was going to have to close The Collector's Exchange.

Since he'd opened up, business had steadily increased, but at such a slow rate that he'd yet to make a profit. Instead, he'd been forced to live and pay a portion of The Collector's Exchange's overhead from his savings.

The trouble was, he'd attracted only the small collectors who weren't likely to spend much. Not that Gabe looked down on that; he understood it. The kids the shop drew weren't big buyers, and braces on a kid's teeth had to take priority over a new baseball card for Dad.

Unfortunately, understanding didn't help pay the bills, let alone give him the kind of profit that allowed him to purchase some of the real finds in this business when he came across them and didn't have a ready buyer.

But now, just as it was looking as if The Collector's Exchange wasn't going to make it into its second year, a new door had opened.

The owner of a shop not far away had retired and recommended Gabe to his customers. Among them was a group of investors who were serious, big-money comic-book collectors—potential buyers for the three original issues of a series called Baby Jack Flash that Adeline just happened to own.

Gabe was scrambling the eggs when the doorbell rang.

"Come on in, it's open," he said, reasonably sure it was his father.

"It's just your old man," Eli Duran called as he opened the screen. At sixty-seven he didn't look a day over fifty-five. He had a full head of wavy white hair, a barely lined face and a spring in his step. But at a scant five foot seven and with an incredible sweet tooth, retirement had put a paunch around his middle that even daily exercise couldn't take away.

"I saw signs of life across the street," Eli said as he joined Gabe in the kitchen. "Adeline's niece?"

Gabe nodded. "Gracie got in late last night."

White eyebrows arched high. "*Gracie,* is it? How did you get so friendly already?"

"I went over to light the water heater."

"Quick work," Eli said slyly.

"I didn't think she'd want to get up this morning and take a cold bath," Gabe answered as if he hadn't heard the insinuation in his father's tone.

"Last time I saw her she was a little girl."

"Well, she isn't a little girl anymore."

"I could tell that by the way you said *Gracie.*" Eli poked Gabe in the side with his elbow.

"Set the table, will you?"

Eli laughed heartily as he gathered dishes, silverware and napkins from the cupboards. "So you liked Addie's niece, did you?"

"Mmm," Gabe answered noncommittally. "She met me at the door wearing feathers in her hair, tacky earrings, bracelets up to her elbows and enough necklaces to look like an Egyptian."

"That sounds like a niece of Addie's."

"She said she'd found a box of stuff she used to play with and couldn't resist it."

"And you thought she was as charming as my Addie," Eli guessed smugly.

Gabe couldn't stop the smile that gave him away. "Yes, I thought she was as charming as *your Addie.* In fact, she seems a lot like Adeline all the way around. She's warm, unpretentious, personable, a little off center. She has a beautiful smile, a terrific laugh, silky hair, big green eyes—'' He realized suddenly how he sounded and stopped. "Anyway, there's no doubt that they're related."

Eli just grinned, showing the perfect white teeth and the gleam in his blue eyes that had won him six wives.

Gabe changed the subject. "She also found an old picture of you and Adeline—looked like you were both wearing horse skulls on your heads like hats."

"The trip to New Mexico! They *were* horse skulls. That was Addie's idea."

"I never had a doubt."

"I haven't even thought about that trip in years. And here she still has pictures," Eli mused, clearly distracted from talking about Gracie, just the way Gabe wanted.

"Of course, Adeline still has the pictures," Gabe said. "You should know better than anyone that she forms sentimental attachments to everything from paper scraps to grass clippings. She never gets rid of anything, let alone old pictures of the two of you on one of your trips together."

"True enough. Your Gracie didn't happen to give you the picture did she?"

"She isn't *my Gracie* and no, she didn't happen to give me the picture."

Eli poured juice, handing a glass to Gabe. "I'd sure like to see it, and any others there are. In fact, I'd love to have some of them."

Gabe turned the omelet out onto a dish and brought it to the table. "That's a joke, right?"

Eli took half and set a piece of toast on the edge of his plate. "Of course, it's not a joke. Would you ask your Gracie if she'd share a few with me?"

A forkful of eggs only made it halfway to Gabe's mouth as he stopped to stare at his father. "Eli Duran,

the man who has been married six times and is notorious
for not hanging on to much of anything, wants some old
pictures? I can't believe it.''

Eli shrugged. ''Addie was the love of my life. And now
that she's gone off on this harebrained 'investment in a
better afterlife' as she called it, I'll never see her again. I'd
like to have some pictures of us together for old times'
sake. Is that so strange?''

''If Adeline was the love of your life why did you
marry six other women and never her?''

''I'd been married three times when I met Addie and
she thought I was a bad risk—not to mention the fact that
her religion didn't recognize divorce and wouldn't con-
done any marriage between us. She refused me anything
but friendship. But we were the best of friends, I'll tell
you.''

''I know, Pop.''

''So, will you ask her niece for some of the pictures?''

Gabe ate a few more bites, staring at his food as he did.
''Ordinarily that wouldn't be a big deal,'' he finally said,
hedging.

''But?''

''I don't want to seem like some kind of scavenger.''

''The comic books,'' Eli guessed.

Gabe nodded. ''The comic books.''

''I don't know why you didn't tell me about your financial problems,'' his father complained.

''I told you why I didn't say anything about The Collector's Exchange being in trouble—I didn't want you to
worry about it.''

''Yes, but if you had told me and let me talk to Adeline—''

''You'd still have worried about it. I wouldn't have told
you after she left except I was sure I was home free.''

"So did you talk to your Gracie about finishing out the deal you started with Addie for those old magazines?"

Gabe got up and brought the coffeepot to the table, topping off both cups before replacing it and sitting back down again. "I was only there a few minutes to light the water heater. We didn't really talk."

"Are you sure selling just those three comics will keep you in business?"

"The commission on them will. In fact, it will keep me going for a long time. But the money isn't the only reason this deal is so important. Getting comics as rare as the Baby Jack Flash will convince this group of investors to let me search for whatever they want in the future and handle their purchases and sales."

"Didn't you already do something for them?"

"I advised them to sell some other, less important issues they owned to raise the capital for Adeline's three."

"And that paid your bills last month, didn't you say?"

"It kept my doors open, yes. But the other bonus to establishing a group like this as steady clients is that word will get around in the big leagues, I'll make more contacts with other collectors of this caliber and also get myself a place in the circles where the really rare collector's editions become available."

"Well, if you'd have told me that you were trying to talk Addie into selling something, I could have helped you out and you would have finished the deal before she left. You'd be sitting pretty right now."

Gabe leaned back in his chair and watched his father finish what was left of the eggs and toast. "How was I supposed to know Adeline was going to get word from the monastery that she'd been accepted and take off like a shot?"

"Did her niece even mention the letter you said Addie sent her about the agreement?"

Gabe scratched his ear. "No, she didn't say anything about it. But as I said, I was only there a few minutes. It was hardly an opportune time to discuss business."

"And you're going back today?"

Gabe nodded. "I called Dave the minute I knew she was here last night and got him to take over for me at the shop. I'm going to show Gracie what she needs to know about Adeline's house."

"And hope the subject of the comics comes up."

"Actually, I've been debating about that. I hate to leave it to chance. But at the same time I don't want to bombard her with it before she's even been able to unpack."

"Well, if you want my opinion, I'd say that unless she brings it up herself, you should wait. She's just come all the way from Australia. Give her a few days to settle in. You don't want to alienate her."

The sly tone was back in his father's voice. But Eli was right. Gabe definitely didn't want to alienate Gracie—and not just for the sake of The Collector's Exchange. "I suppose I'll hold off. As anxious as I am to get my hands on those comics, I wouldn't want to do anything to blow it. I *can't* do anything to blow it. I have too much riding on this deal."

"And the fact that Addie left the comics to Gracie, and you have to work with her now isn't going to be too painful for you, is it?" Eli asked facetiously.

Gabe couldn't help but grin at his father. "Yeah, okay, so I'll be glad to see her," he admitted.

His father didn't have to know just how glad.

Standing at the picture window in the living room, Gracie savored her first cup of hot lemon water and the lingering image of Gabe Duran in his underwear. She hadn't seen a man in his underwear since Burt and she felt a little guilty about it. Well, not guilty about having seen Gabe—that was his own fault for going outside like that—but she did feel guilty about how much she'd enjoyed the sight.

And she had definitely enjoyed the sight. Nice. Very nice. Nice enough to be still vividly in her mind even long after Gabe had gone back inside and she'd seen his father arrive.

Gabe's body without shirt and pants was everything it promised to be when dressed. His shoulders were broad, his chest was wide and just brawny enough to look powerful without being overly pumped up. His arms were visions of well-defined muscles, his waist was narrow, his belly flat, and those legs—long and sinewy and hard looking—made up for his slightly knobby knees. All in all, the body went very well with the face.

Then he'd looked up and realized she'd seen him in only his shorts. "Turnabout is fair play, neighbor," she said at the memory, toasting his house. "Now we've both seen each other in a less than dignified getup."

Once he'd realized she was watching he hadn't flaunted his infinitely flauntable body or jumped back into the house as if he had something to hide. He'd waved and smiled a little smile that said he was embarrassed to be caught in the act but didn't take himself or the situation too seriously. Gracie liked that.

She liked him.

And for a moment that made her catch her breath.

She closed her eyes and explored the feelings she was having as if trying on old clothes to see if they still fit. Lord, but it was strange to be attracted to a man who wasn't Burt.

There had been times in the past six months when she'd wondered if she would ever feel anything for another man again. After all, she loved Burt and that hadn't just disappeared when he died.

But it had changed, she realized. Somewhere along the path of these six months it had tucked itself away into a corner of her heart and turned into a part of the past.

She was glad of that. When the love was active it had been so hard to face that he was gone. There had been so many times when what was in her heart made it impossible for her to accept what she knew in her head was the truth. So many mornings when in those first few moments of waking she'd forgotten he was dead and only woke wondering why he wasn't in bed with her.

But that didn't happen anymore. In fact, it hadn't happened in a couple of months. It had gone the way of the constant tears, the horrible anger, the numbing reality of facing life without him.

And what was she left with now that she'd come through so many of the stages of grief?

Peace. And acceptance.

Thank God.

She'd been crazy for a while. Right after the incident happened. She hadn't been herself. She hadn't been able to concentrate, to think straight, to remember why she'd begun to say something by the time she was finished saying it. Some days she'd had more energy than ten people. Other days she couldn't get out of bed. What gave her pleasure and solace one moment had made her cry the next.

That was when the job in Australia had come up. More than a career opportunity, it had been an escape from the sudden chaos of Burt's death.

At any other time, Gracie probably wouldn't have accepted the job and the upheaval of it. But then it had seemed like a way out, a retreat from memories, from the city, the people, the routines she and Burt had shared.

And Australia had been all of that. It had given her the time and space and distance she needed. It had offered her a sense of being disconnected that had allowed her to deal with her grief without being eaten alive by it. It had let her heal herself.

And she was healed. She'd known it the day she'd received the news of what her aunt was doing. At that moment she'd found in herself the desire to go back to a place in which she had roots, a craving for the stability and continuity she'd always needed before Burt's death. And those old desires and cravings had told her clearly that she was back to herself again.

But thoughts like the ones she was having about Gabe as she stood at the window still seemed strange and disloyal.

"It's just too soon for it," she told herself out loud, as if the sound of her own voice, the reasoning in her tone, would chase the attraction away.

But there it stayed with his image firmly in her mind and her eyes focused on his house as if just waiting to catch another sight of him.

"Time to get going, Gracie," she ordered, spinning around and taking her cup into the kitchen with the determination of a platoon sergeant.

The lack of a dishwasher was a big negative she intended to rectify as soon as possible, she decided in an effort to keep her thoughts on the straight and narrow as she washed and dried the cup, putting it back in the cupboard where she'd found it. Then she began opening and closing all the rest of the cupboard doors to judge what kind of space she had for her own things.

In the process she found a jar of Adeline's potpourri. She opened it and sniffed. Cinnamon and orange. And it was still potent—her aunt must have mixed it not long before she'd left.

Gracie had seen enough to know there was no room at all for her kitchen things without doing some major sorting and rearranging. So, rather than go through any more cupboards, she took the jar of potpourri down.

Setting out her "sachets" was something Adeline had done for company. To hold the potpourri, she'd used tiny china plates covered with red rosebuds. They were part of a tea set that had been Adeline's when she was a little girl, and Gracie went in search of them in the dining-room sideboard.

She found them right where they'd been the last time her aunt had sent her for them—the left-hand section of the carved oak sideboard with the silver chafing dish in the center of it. The sideboard matched the huge oval table where Gracie set out the dishes to be filled. As she did she glanced at the six Windsor chairs that completed the set, remembering innumerable holiday dinners shared there.

It was the smell of the potpourri, she thought, that brought back such vivid memories. And she was happy to have them. They were part of what she loved about this house—the memories and the stories every scratch told.

Taking the tiny dishes of the spice and fruit peels into every room, she took a mental inventory of all she loved about this place. The way the winter wind whistled through the oak window frames, the rich shadows cast by thick velvet drapes pulled back over French lace sheers, the sound of Sunday shoes on the genuine hardwood floors, the crackle of fires in the hearths in the living, dining and bedrooms that once upon a time were the only sources of heat.

What was there not to love in the dining room's bay window of stained glass, whose yellow glow of diffused light always felt like sunshine to Gracie? Or the hand-carved spandrels that made ornate arches out of plain square entryways—the perfect places to hang mistletoe at Christmastime?

With sachets in every room on the lower level, Gracie took the rest upstairs, picturing the satin ribbons that Adeline had wound around the banister on Gracie's wedding day.

In the children's room—as her aunt had always called the front bedroom—Gracie set one of the tiny plates on the nightstand that separated the matching brass youth beds with the old trunks at the foot of each. She and Willy had spent more nights than she could count whispering and giggling on their sleepovers with Aunt Adeline. And the only time they'd gotten into any real trouble was when they'd had a jumping contest on the big bed in the master suite to see who could get the closest to the top of the eight-foot mahogany headboard—the bed that was now Gracie's—and nearly broken the Tiffany lamp beside it with its leaded-glass pattern of bluebells.

She loved this place, all right, Gracie thought as she took the last sachet into the bathroom that had been converted from a third bedroom when the plumbing had been installed.

The attic didn't extend over this room, so the entire ceiling of glass supported by wooden beams gave it the atmosphere and the advantages of an old, elegant greenhouse—or conservatory, as Adeline was wont to call it.

Four wooden windows made up one wall, and vines grew heartily up the frames and onto the beams. The pedestal sink and toilet stood unobtrusively in an alcove off the main room where a ceiling-high armoire stood against the inside wall. A vanity and mirror took up a third wall, and a claw-footed tub stood between two oak Tuscan columns around which more vines wrapped themselves.

Setting the last plate of potpourri on the vanity, Gracie started her bathwater. "No, I wouldn't trade this place for anything."

Except maybe some hot water.

Shortly before one that afternoon, when Gabe was due to come over, Gracie went across the street to his house to head him off.

A ranch-style home, it was redbrick, L-shaped, and trimmed in black and white with a steep shake-shingle roof. The entrance faced the street and on the small stoop in front of it Gracie found a huge chocolate-colored dog lying with his head between two fat, velvety paws. The animal greeted her with nothing more than a single raised eyebrow.

"Are you friendly?" she asked as she approached.

Gabe's laugh answered her from inside the screen. "Murf is a lazy old bag of bones. He wouldn't hurt a soul."

He also wouldn't move even when the screen door gently nudged his hind end. Instead, the animal closed his eyes as if he hadn't noticed a thing.

"Move it, Murf," Gabe ordered in the affectionate tone of voice he might have used with a stubborn old codger he was fond of in spite of it all.

With his eyes still closed, Murf groaned a complaint and dropped one hip to the concrete. Gabe opened the door as far as he could, which wasn't much. "A little more, Murf."

This time the animal lumbered to his feet, cast an accusing eye to Gracie and walked off.

"Sorry. He's old as dirt and cantankerous as they come," Gabe said as he held the door open for her. "I was just on my way over."

"I wanted to catch you before you left so I could call the phone company and set up an installation time."

"Good idea."

He showed her to a cordless phone on an end table as stark looking as a walnut building block. She dialed and a machine answered, asking her to hold. While she waited she watched Gabe check his mail.

His hair shone with coffee-colored highlights. It was neater than it had been the night before, but the top still had a slightly mussed look to it—something that said he'd combed it but not carefully or meticulously. It suited him, she thought.

He wore a red crewneck T-shirt with no room to spare across the breadth of his chest and shoulders. The long sleeves were pushed above his elbows and she noticed the thickness of his forearms and wrists before her gaze wandered to the snug jeans that traced his hips and thighs. In her mind's eye she could see what was beneath the clothes as clearly as she'd seen him this morning.

She glanced down at the brown shag carpeting but still the vivid image lingered, and when a phone employee's voice finally came on the line she was grateful for the distraction.

It didn't take long to arrange for the installation, and then Gracie and Gabe went back to her house just as the moving truck drove up.

"Finally. They were supposed to be here first thing this morning."

"Big truck," Gabe observed of the long yellow-and-green semi towing a small car. "It isn't full, is it?"

"Almost," Gracie answered ruefully.

"Where are you going to put it all? That house is brimming with stuff as it is."

"I know. I'm not sure what I'm going to do with all my things. For now I'll have to store them in the garage and little by little I guess I'll merge the two households."

"Good luck," Gabe said dubiously.

Gracie explained to the movers that she wanted her television, tape player, stereo and microwave in the house and the rest in the garage—actually, what had originally been a carriage house. Then she took Gabe inside.

"This time instead of lighting the pilot light you'd better show me how to do it. I had a cold bath this morning in spite of your best intentions last night." Gracie refrained from adding that it had probably been just what she needed after seeing Gabe in his underwear.

"Let's start there, then," he suggested.

It wasn't easy for Gracie to keep her mind on what he was teaching her as her gaze strayed to little details about him—the way his hair brushed the top of his ears, the thickness of his neck, corded and strong looking, the narrowness of his waist.

But she battled the distraction and tried to concentrate as he went from showing her how to light the pilot light to pointing out the fuse box and the jar full of fuses that Adeline kept on a shelf with the laundry detergent.

"The furnace has to be primed and oiled, and sometimes kicked, to work—but I think it would be better for me to show you that when the weather cools off. Just don't let me forget to talk to you about keeping the damper open on it when I do."

"Okay," she agreed.

From there they moved to the back door that opened off the rear kitchen wall. In order to close it securely it had to be slammed and then pressed with a foot at the bottom for the dead bolt to work.

He demonstrated how to latch the small box freezer inside the ancient refrigerator that barely reached to Gracie's shoulder. Then she moved to the equally old gas stove.

"I lit one of these burners this morning to heat water and nearly scorched my eyeballs—is there a trick to it?"

Gabe nodded and smiled. "Keep your eyeballs out of the way."

Gracie laughed, but she wasn't thrilled to hear that her experience was common to lighting all the burners and that there was nothing she could do about it.

"This can't be opened," he said, pointing to the large window over the kitchen table. "The frame is cracked and rather than having it replaced Adeline just nailed it shut."

Gabe then led the way into the small bathroom off the kitchen. Nothing at all like the wide-open, beautiful bath upstairs, this one was only a toilet and a sink in a space that wouldn't have made a good closet.

In the tiny room Gabe was near enough for Gracie to smell his after-shave and for a moment her mind wandered again. Then a shrieking whistle snapped her out of it.

Gabe had turned on the tap in the sink and water burst out like a geyser. Shouting over the noise, he said, "I don't know what you do about this, but since you're going to have to call a plumber for the toilet down here you'd better have him take a look at the sink, too."

Grimacing at the sound, Gracie didn't answer until he turned the tap off and she didn't have to scream to be heard. "I'll definitely have the sink looked at," she assured him.

"You should also talk to him about some kind of insulation for the water pipes. They freeze almost every winter."

"Something else my aunt liked?" she asked with a laugh.

"No, but she took it in her stride and put off doing anything to prevent it."

"Adeline—the great procrastinator."

"The greatest."

As they went through the living room he warned her not to use the fireplaces until she had a chimney sweep take a look at them. Before going up the stairs he pulled off the newel cap on the banister to demonstrate that it was just sitting there, unattached.

On the upper level he showed her how to close the hall closet door by lifting up on it before pushing it shut. Then he opened it again to explain that the piles of what looked like cloth snakes were used to block winter air and moisture from coming in through all the windowsills and the thresholds. "Otherwise, about two inches of pure ice forms."

He warned her that the roof leaked in some rooms, and explained that all the electrical outlets sparked if there were more than one plug in them; the outside gutters had to have leaves cleaned out of them at least twice a year because of the giant trees that lined the property, their branches reaching toward the house; and the roots of those same trees had a tendency to clog the sewer pipes.

"And Adeline told me to tell you to be especially careful of the light switch in the front bedroom—it has a short in it and sometimes if you hit it just right you'll get a little jolt," he finished.

"Is that all?" Gracie joked.

"No, that's just for starters. I was saving the really big things for after you're settled in," he teased back. Then he seemed to study her, frowning curiously. "Do you really like this old place the way Adeline thought?"

"I'm crazy about it."

Gabe just shook his head in amazement as they went back downstairs and outside.

They spent the remainder of the afternoon helping to unload the truck and then setting up the few things Gracie was taking into the house for now.

Passing each other on one trip after another, they didn't have time for too much conversation. Instead, they began trading quips and teasing each other. Before too long it felt as if she'd known him forever and Gracie reveled in the easy rapport that was developing between them.

It was early evening by the time the movers left. As Gracie thanked them and set the front screen door back in the frame to close it, Gabe plugged her stereo into a socket on the wall beside the stairs. Then he took a good look at the antique cabinet that encased the system and appeared for all the world as nothing more than a sideboard.

"Even your modern conveniences are camouflaged," he marveled.

"I did that piece myself," she told him. "There was no back to it and the insides were beyond repair but I knew I could bring the top, sides and front back to life, so I gutted it and added what I needed to hold the stereo."

"Ever thought of buying a nice, new cabinet?"

She gave him an exaggerated look of shock. "And do what with this fine, aged work of cabinetry?"

"Junk it?"

"You sound just like Willy. I would never do that. New things don't have any character—not to mention that they aren't built the way old ones are."

"But they come with their own insides," he said as if trying to tempt her.

She made a face and shook her head. "Not worth it." Then she glanced at her watch and changed the subject. "Dinnertime. Can I treat you to a pizza as payment for services rendered above and beyond the call of duty?"

"Can it be fresh or do you like your pizza old and stale like your houses and furniture?"

"Fresh, definitely fresh."

"Then I'll take you up on your offer. I'll go home and order it, feed Murf and wash my hands. I should get back over here about the same time the pizza does."

Gracie knew her smile was too big, but she couldn't help it. Even after the hours they'd already been together, she was loath to lose his company and pleased that she wouldn't have to. Not yet, anyway. "Sounds good to me."

Half an hour later the pizza arrived, but Gabe wasn't back yet. Gracie knew Adeline would have had a fit but she ignored the kitchen table and set the box in the center of the dining-room table, anyway. Her aunt had held firmly to the notion that the dining room was only for formal or family dinners, not for eating pizza out of the box. But Gracie didn't care.

She'd gone upstairs and changed out of her moving-day sweat suit and into a pair of clean jeans and a crisp white blouse, pinning a brooch at her throat and turning the collar up around her jawbone—a style she usually reserved for a somewhat fancier occasion, a movie at least. But somehow she couldn't fight the sense that even just sharing a pizza with Gabe to repay him for his help was something special.

The feeling was probably a little dangerous, coming now, so soon after Burt's death and at a time when she knew she must be particularly vulnerable. It was probably something she shouldn't indulge in.

But in six months she hadn't primped for any reason, and wanting to again felt good.

So the dining room it was.

Gabe had apparently done a little primping of his own, she thought when he rang the doorbell five minutes later. He'd changed into a sport shirt—pale yellow and crisp. The shade set off his swarthy coloring but somehow Gracie was a little disappointed that the shirt didn't cup his muscular torso the way his T-shirt had.

"Good timing. The pizza just got here."

"Great. I'm starving."

She led the way to the dining room. "So tell me how you got to know my aunt," she said as she served the pizza.

"I'd met her a couple of times as a kid, with my father. But we didn't become friends until I bought the house across the street. That was three years ago. You know Adeline—she took me under her wing, as she called it. Introduced me to the neighbors, fed me, invited me to play chess with her—do you play, by the way?"

"Would any niece of Adeline's not?"

He smiled at her. "Great. We'll have to play. Anyway, she and I just hit it off. But then, Adeline hit it off with everybody." He finished his first slice of pizza and helped himself to a second. "What about you? You and your aunt must have been close for her to have left you all she did—even if I didn't ever get to meet you."

Was he flirting with her? It had been a long time and Gracie wasn't sure. But it seemed like it. Especially when he was smiling that warm honey smile again and looking right into her eyes. "I was here all the time as a kid. It was my second home. Even when I got older I'd visit whenever Adeline wasn't off on one of her trips. But then I got married and moved to Connecticut. I couldn't get back here much, so she came to stay with me."

"She talked about you all the time."

"Did she?" Gracie laughed. "She probably told you all my deepest, darkest secrets."

"Adeline? You know better than that. Nobody can keep a confidence the way she can. It drove my father crazy. He said he always had the feeling she knew things he didn't."

"Oh, I don't know about Adeline keeping anything from your father. She was pretty crazy about him."

"He was pretty crazy about her, too. In fact, he surprised me this morning talking about her. He said she was the love of his life, but that she wouldn't marry him because he'd been divorced three times by the time they met."

"She called him The Rogue," Gracie confided with the same slightly scandalized, slightly fascinated tone of voice her aunt would have used.

"That's my father, all right. He played the field so much before he met my mother you'd think he would have gotten it out of his system. But so far there've been five wives since their divorce and who knows how many more he might have.'' Gabe took a drink of iced tea. ''Not that I'm saying anything against him. He's a good guy—generous and bighearted. He just likes women and they like him.''

Like father, like son? Gracie could only vouch for the part about the women appreciating Gabe, because she definitely did.

''How did you like Australia?'' he asked.

''It wasn't home, but it was a fascinating place. And the work was interesting.''

''Back to all that old stuff again,'' he teased. ''I'd think you'd get tired of it—working with it, living with it—''

''Don't you have any appreciation for classic beauty?''

He looked squarely at her and smiled a rakish half smile. ''Beauty I appreciate,'' he said pointedly. ''But old is just old.''

Gracie was embarrassed by the veiled compliment and didn't know what to say to it. She also didn't know how to stop from blushing—something she hadn't done since she was a teenager.

But then he spared her more embarrassment by going on. ''So, how did you decide to do this for a living?''

''My dad and Willy's are brothers and cabinetmakers. Mine did a lot of antique refurbishing on the side and I loved to watch him work. As I got older he started having me help and my doing it as a job just evolved from there.''

''But I understand you're very good at it—good enough for museums and archives to hire.''

''My aunt was bragging, I take it? I just have a lot of patience when it comes to sanding wood down to its nat-

ural state, and I get a big charge out of being able to du-
plicate a missing leg or spindle or whatever. I'm lucky to
be able to make a living doing something I love."

"And your brother sells antiques, is that right?"

"He has a store across town."

Gracie felt as if she was monopolizing the conversation and, since they were finished eating, she stood and
took the pizza box to the kitchen.

"I can't offer you anything fancy for dessert but I do
have a couple of chocolate bars, if you're interested," she
said on the way.

"It isn't chocolate bars I'm interested in," he said
somewhat under his breath as he followed her into the
kitchen with their plates and glasses.

Gracie definitely didn't know what to say to that. Or
if she was even meant to hear it. So while she put soap
and water in the sink to wash the dishes, she said, "Did
you tell your father we found a picture of him last
night?"

Gabe opened a drawer and took out a tea towel as if he
were in his own home. As he waited for the first dish he
turned his back to the counter and leaned against it. His
hip was near Gracie's. And Gracie was very conscious of
it. It didn't seem possible, but she felt as though she could
feel the heat of his body through his clothes and hers.

"As a matter of fact, I did talk to him about the picture. That was how he got into the subject of his feelings
for Adeline—he asked me to ask you if you would think
about letting him have an old snapshot or two of them
together."

Gracie washed the first dish, rinsed it and handed it to
him, much too aware of the sight of his long, thick fingers taking it from her. The second dish got scrubbed

harder than the first. "Sure. If I know my aunt she has hundreds of pictures of them together around here someplace. When I come across them your father can have whatever he wants—I'm sure they don't count as the things she's trusted me not to part with."

"Did she put that in her will—that she was trusting you not to part with anything?"

"Absolutely. That was the reason she left me what she did."

Gabe didn't say anything as he put the first plate in the cupboard. Then, taking the second dish from her he said, "Pop will be glad to hear you won't mind parting with some of the pictures. I'll tell him tomorrow morning when we walk."

"When you walk?"

"My father and Murf and I do about four miles every morning—summer and winter. I used to jog but neither one of them could keep up with that and it was bad on my knees and ankles, so I switched. I do a few more miles a week than I did running, and I think it evens out." He folded the towel and hung it on a bar inside the cupboard below the sink. Then he glanced at the schoolhouse clock on the wall. "I better get going."

But he didn't move and Gracie felt something in the air between them. Maybe because he was so close beside her, or maybe because she could smell his after-shave again, or maybe she'd just gone insane, but it suddenly seemed as if there were some sort of electricity flashing from him to her.

She spun away and headed for the front door, opening it for him once she got there. "I really appreciate all your help today," she said, looking up into those unusual blue eyes of his.

"No problem. Thanks for the pizza."

"It was nothing." Gracie told herself to quit staring at him, but she went right on, anyway. She had the oddest sensation—as if that same electrical force that she'd felt in the kitchen was holding her to him now, too.

"Do you think you can light the water heater when it goes out again?"

"Sure." Was his voice softer, deeper, almost raspy? Or was she just imagining it?

"Well, if you need me—for anything, even if it's in the middle of the night—just holler."

"Thanks, I will." And why was her own voice so breathy?

Still Gabe stayed there, staring back at her. She saw his gaze slide down her nose and touch her lips; she even had the sense that she could feel it.

She swallowed, wondering if he was going to kiss her. And it didn't seem awkward—not at all the way she'd imagined her first kiss by anyone but Burt to be. It seemed perfectly natural. Natural enough for her to tip her chin up just a little.

But instead of coming nearer Gabe stood up straighter than he'd been before, and a muscle tightened in his jaw. "Good night, Gracie," he said quietly, and then he left before she had even thought to answer him.

She watched him cross the street. And she felt a twinge of something she shouldn't be feeling.

It was good that he hadn't kissed her, she told herself. What could she have been thinking? She'd just met this man. She didn't even know him. She didn't even know what he did for a living. Certainly she shouldn't be kissing him.

But if he had tried she'd have let him.

And somewhere deep down inside she couldn't help being disappointed that he hadn't.

Chapter Three

"It's about time," Gracie said to herself when the doorbell rang the next morning. She didn't have a doubt that it was the telephone installer, who was already two hours late.

She climbed down from the chair she was standing on to sort through cupboards, wiping her hands on the thighs of her grey sweat suit as she went to the door.

On the front porch was the phone man, all right—she could tell by the tool belt riding low on his jeans-encased hips. He was tall and knock-'em-dead gorgeous. Between his face and the muscular torso that nearly bulged out of his green T-shirt, Gracie thought he looked more like a male dancer in disguise—Frank the Phone Man. If loud music had started to play and he'd begun to strip off his clothes she wouldn't have been surprised.

"You need some phone work done?" he asked through the screen when she opened the door.

"Sure do," she said as she held the screen for him as she'd done for Gabe that first night here.

The man was much the same size as Gabe, so he came just as close when he stepped over the threshold, but rather than noticing the scent of after-shave, Gracie only felt vaguely uncomfortable.

"The old phone was in the kitchen." She pointed toward the rear of the house. "But I'm going to want the bedroom upstairs wired, too."

"Let's see what we have down here, first," the man said, not waiting for Gracie to show him the way.

She came up behind him as he found the hole in the kitchen wall and pulled the old wires farther out. He was no slouch in the looks department from the back, either, she thought. And yet...

Somehow the man's looks had no effect on her.

She kept comparing him with Gabe and finding Gabe more attractive, when in truth this guy was even better looking. Very strange.

Gabe's personality and sense of humor had an influence, she reasoned. And the fact that she found it so easy to talk to him.

But there was something more, too, and she didn't quite understand it.

She'd met Burt her first week of high school and though she'd thought he was a nice enough guy, that was all she'd thought about him. Even when he'd asked her out and she'd accepted, she hadn't felt particularly bowled over by him—it was just a date. Liking him, loving him, had grown slowly and over time as she'd gotten to know him.

Compared to that, the intense attraction she felt for Gabe seemed pretty weird. Especially when it even negated appreciation for a hunk like the phone man.

"You're all set down here. Can you show me where you need the upstairs extension?" He interrupted her thoughts when he'd finished his work in the kitchen.

"Sure." Gracie led the way to her bedroom, realizing only as she did how long she'd been lost in thoughts of Gabe.

The installer went right to work once he knew where she wanted the second phone and for a moment Gracie again watched him. He was a man any red-blooded woman would drool over. And he didn't have the slightest effect on her.

But one glance out the window at Gabe's house was all it took for her heartbeat to speed up.

Maybe this reaction to Gabe was just a reawakening. There were stages of grief and she'd passed through them all. But what if a sudden, strong attraction to a new person was a stage the self-help books just didn't go far enough to mention? Was it really so odd that it would happen with a man who had been kind and friendly to her, as opposed to some handsome stranger? It didn't seem odd. In fact, it seemed pretty healthy. Maybe she should take it as a good sign—nature giving notice that she really was still alive and well and kicking.

It was possible. And after all, what was wrong with a little innocent appreciation of her neighbor? Okay, so maybe she was particularly vulnerable so soon after Burt's death, but it wasn't as if she was jumping into a relationship with Gabe. She was just feeling appreciative of his looks, his personality, his mannerisms, his company. Nothing wrong with that.

"If you don't need me I'll go back downstairs," she told the phone man.

He said that was fine, and, feeling much better, she left him alone in the bedroom.

When the installer had finished and left, Gracie temporarily postponed working on the kitchen cupboards. The first thing she did was call her brother's number. She didn't expect Dean to be there but she wanted to leave a message on his machine so he'd know how to reach her.

Then she dialed Willy at work.

"I'm calling you from my very own phone," Gracie told her cousin without saying hello.

"Great," Willy answered. Then she said, "Hang on a minute, will you, Gracie?"

Gracie said she would. As she waited her gaze drifted down the hallway beside the stairs, out the front door and to Gabe's house just as his garage door opened and he backed his car out.

She couldn't see many details at that distance, just his dark hair, his long right arm stretched across the top of the seat, his profile as he turned to make sure there were no other cars coming. But that was all it took to send a little shiver of delight up her spine. Only this time instead of questioning it she just enjoyed it.

"Okay, I'm back. No rest for the wicked," Willy said when she came on the line again.

"No rest for receptionists in busy dentists' offices, either."

"I can talk now, though. I handed over the reins to the hygienist for a minute. How's it going?"

"Good. My phone was just hooked up and I thought I'd call and give you my number."

"Okay, shoot. I'll write it on my hand so I won't forget to take it home with me tonight."

Gracie read the number from the little window below the push buttons.

"Seen any more of your cute neighbor since the other night?" Willy asked.

"He came over yesterday, showed me how to work stuff around here and then helped unload the moving truck."

"Lucky you."

True enough. Or at least that was how Gracie felt. "Then I bought him a pizza as payment." She almost added that she thought Gabe had nearly kissed her good-night, too, but stopped herself before she went that far.

"So you had dinner together," Willy said, her tone insinuating something more.

"Just pizza," Gracie repeated as if the food had been more important than the company when in fact that hadn't been true. The evening had felt like a date. A nice date. But somehow saying that to Willy seemed a step beyond the silent attraction Gracie had just decided she could be comfortable with. "Anyway, all my stuff is here."

"What did you do with everything?"

"Most of it is jammed in the garage. I started today to try sorting and organizing to make room. I'm headed for the attic as soon as we hang up, to see what I can put there."

"Good luck," Willy said as if it was hopeless.

"It won't be so bad."

"I don't care what Adeline said in her will, I think you're going to have to chuck some of her junk."

"I can't do that."

"You could. She'd never know the difference."

"I'd know. And I won't do it. She trusted me and that's all there is to it."

"Which leaves you back at square one—where are you going to put your own things?"

"I'll figure something out. I better let you get back to work."

"Talk to you soon. If you need me, holler."

Gracie hung up and headed for the attic, hoping to find storage space. What she found was everything but.

One big, open room, the attic was stocked with what Adeline had amassed over the years. Not that it was just tossed haphazardly up here. It was all neatly shelved, stacked and organized.

Old clothes and shoes, knickknacks, chipped china, scratched silver, hats of every color and shape, shelves and shelves of books, more still of home movies and photograph albums. There was a box marked "Soap dishes from around the world"—souvenirs Adeline had brought back from her travels—and another tagged "Hummels." There were school pennants, Halloween costumes, jewelry boxes, baseball caps and three bats, fruit bowls, canning jars, an iron teapot, splattered tin dishes, pots and pans, a milk can and even an old chamber pot.

And that was just along one of the four walls.

Gracie turned slowly to look at the other three without mentally cataloging what was stored there. No matter what the contents, the fact was there was very little space that would allow her to add anything from downstairs. Scratch that idea.

Somehow she hadn't expected every nook and cranny of this house to be so full. Foolish of her, she supposed, but she'd thought she would be able to rearrange, organize and restack to make room to add her household to Adeline's.

"Well," she said with a resigned sigh, "I can't get rid of any of it." So organizing, restacking and rearranging were going to have to work.

Knowing the attic would not allow immediate relief, she decided to head back to the kitchen to see what kind of magic she could work there, after all.

As she passed the attic shelf that held the albums with Adeline's favorite photographs in them, though, she remembered that Gabe's father had asked for some of the snapshots. She grabbed several of them and took them with her. Giving away a couple of pictures wasn't going to gain her any space but it was the only thing of Adeline's she felt comfortable parting with.

Gabe watched his customer walk out of the store after his purchase of four baseball cards. Total sale: six dollars. And it was the biggest one he'd made all day.

"So, what do you want for a Wednesday?" he asked himself.

Not that Monday and Tuesday had been much better.

But there was comfort in knowing things were about to change.

He rounded the counter where he displayed the more valuable cards, comics and coins, so he could reslot the magazines two boys had looked at earlier. Pulling one of the comics out of the wrong rack pocket exposed a copy of a young love series aimed at teenagers in the sixties. The cover had an elaborate drawing of a bathing-suit-clad girl on the verge of being soundly kissed by a lifeguard.

That was all it took to make Gabe think about the previous night. Or to be more precise, the way the previous night had almost ended.

He'd come close to kissing Gracie. Very close. In fact, he couldn't remember wanting anything quite as badly as he'd wanted to kiss her. At least, not since he was a hormone-crazed teenager.

And that struck him as a little strange.

After all, he wasn't a teenager. He was old enough and had enough experience with women—not to mention enough lessons in his father's hasty marriages—to have learned that getting to know a woman before leaping into a relationship had a lot to recommend it.

But that hadn't mattered last night.

Spending the day with her had taken his initial interest in her firmly into the bounds of attraction. He was a sucker for the way the sun shot polished copper streaks through her hair, for the sight of her rear end as she climbed the porch steps. The soft sound of her laugh had left him inclined to make a fool of himself just to hear it again, and being the recipient of her quick wit and teasing returns had made a pleasure out of the chore of unloading a moving truck.

Then dinner and finding she was so easy to be alone with, that he was so comfortable with her, had only added to the rest of the attraction. It left him feeling as if he knew her better than he did. Maybe that was why his usual slow courting pace had done a fast forward.

But whatever the reason, he'd wanted that lady last night. So much that for a minute he'd forgotten that they needed to do business together.

It wasn't a good idea to start a relationship—at any pace—before he wrapped up the deal on the comics. He didn't want either one influencing the other.

But once the deal was done? Now that was another story altogether.

Gracie was definitely a woman he wanted to get to know better. And luckily it shouldn't take long to get the comics, turn them over to his customers and have the whole deal behind him so he could do just that.

The phone rang and Gabe went back around the counter to answer it. "The Collector's Exchange."

"Gabe Duran," the male voice on the other end demanded in a peremptory tone.

"This is Gabe Duran."

"This is Gunther Simonesque."

Gunther Simonesque was a member of the group of collectors who wanted the Baby Jack Flash comics. He was a practicing attorney as well as the legal representative for the group. Gabe had met him only twice before, when Simonesque had delivered the receipts and transfer of ownership papers for the magazines the group had sold in order to raise money to buy Adeline's issues.

Gabe liked the other three members of the group—they were all friendly and down-to-earth. But Simonesque was something else again.

"Gunther. What can I do for you?" Gabe said with a note of the same arrogance in his own voice—fighting fire with fire.

"The group met for dinner last night and we discussed the Baby Jack Flash issues."

"Did you?"

"It was decided that I should let you know that we're concerned."

"I'm sorry to hear that," Gabe said as if he couldn't imagine what might be on their minds, careful not to sound the slightest bit anxious. He'd dealt with men like Simonesque in the corporate world and he knew better than to give them an inch. "What concerns you?"

"It's been some time since you began to negotiate for those magazines on our behalf."

"Yes, it has."

"In fact, it's been five weeks since you convinced us to sell the other issues out of our collection."

"I'm aware of that, as well. I handled the sale."

"And made quite a good commission off it."

Gabe didn't answer what was obviously a jab. Instead, he just waited for Simonesque to come to the point.

"We're concerned that after all this time we're no closer to actually owning the comics you offered us—the reason we sold the others in the first place."

"I can understand that. But, as I'm sure you know, sometimes negotiations can take time."

"We were under the impression that a price had been settled on. But that was over three weeks ago and yet we still don't have the comics."

"I've spoken to two of your members in the past three weeks and explained the holdup to them."

"They weren't exactly clear on the problem. We'd appreciate it if you would explain it to me—for the record."

That sounded like a threat but Gabe refused to be intimidated. "Just as we were about to close the sale, Adeline unexpectedly left the country and had her will enacted. As a result the comics were left to her niece, who was in Australia at the time."

Simonesque cut in before Gabe could go on. "And did you make an effort to contact this niece?"

"It was my understanding that the niece was coming back here to accept the inheritance—which involved a great deal more than the Baby Jack Flash comics. I opted for waiting until she arrived to begin negotiations with her."

"And when will that be?"

"She got here on Monday night."

"I see. And how are the negotiations going?"

Gabe was not thrilled to answer that, but he didn't let his reluctance sound in his voice. "I haven't approached her yet. I thought I would give her a few days to settle in first."

"And why is that?"

It wasn't easy to hang on to his patience or his temper, but Gabe managed, if a little tightly. "In my judgment it was for the best. Don't misinterpret the delay, Gunther. The sale will go through as planned. Adeline wrote to her niece explaining her intentions and I have no doubt her niece will comply."

"If she had the time to write to her niece why didn't she just complete the sale on her own?" Simonesque asked with a suspicious note in his voice.

Gabe ignored it. "Adeline thought that going through with the sale would complicate the disposition of her will. Her cash assets were going to someone else and once she sold the comics that money became part of the cash assets. She didn't think it was fair to her niece to do that at the last minute, and there was not time to alter her will so that the money from the comics was treated differently from the rest."

Simonesque didn't say anything.

Gabe knew the lawyer's silence was meant to unnerve him and he refused to let it. Instead, he allowed it to drag on until the other man spoke again.

"The group feels as if you've wasted enough of our time."

"*I* have not wasted any of your time. This is an unforeseen glitch in the deal that's completely out of my control."

"You could have contacted the niece as soon as she arrived in this country."

Gabe was glad the man didn't know Gracie lived right across the street. "Yes, I could have," he agreed. "But in my opinion that served no beneficial purpose. Keep in mind that while Adeline tentatively approved your last offer, she may well have left it to her niece to decide whether or not to actually accept it or to go on negotiating. We wouldn't want to push her into playing hardball, now would we?"

"I see," Simonesque said. "Then when do you think we can expect to finalize this sale?"

"I can't say."

"Then you expect this to go on indefinitely."

Gabe came close to losing the grip on his temper. "No, that's not what I expect," he said slowly, as if that was the only way Simonesque would understand him. "I expect the sale to go through, one way or another, sooner or later. But I can't give you a definite timetable."

"And you'll keep us informed," the other man said snidely.

"Of course, I'll keep you informed."

Simonesque's only response was to hang up.

Gabe followed suit. The he placed both his palms on the countertop, locked his elbows and dropped his head between his shoulders, shaking it as he did.

Simonesque was a bastard. But that bastard was part of a group whose business Gabe needed. And so long as he was dealing with any of the other men in the group his association with them was pleasant.

And okay, maybe they did have reason for concern. After all, this deal had dragged on much longer than it should have because of Adeline's last-minute retreat to Tibet and waiting for Gracie to come back from Australia. But there was nothing Gabe could do about that.

He raised his head and glanced at the clock above the door that led to his storeroom. Another hour to closing.

And then he had to go to Gracie and talk about the comics. Whether she was settled in or not, the whole tone of the phone call had let him know he couldn't afford to wait any longer.

But there was one good thing about rushing Gracie. At least once this deal for the comics was out of the way he could get to know her. Slowly. Steadily. Over time.

It was just after nine o'clock that evening when Gracie's doorbell rang. She was standing on the countertop in the kitchen in order to reach the highest row of cupboards and she considered just not answering the door. But then she realized that the front drapes were open and whoever was on the porch could see that the lights were on in the kitchen, living room, hallway and entrance.

Hanging on to the refrigerator, she did a contortion that allowed her to see down the hallway and out the glass to the front door. Gabe.

Pleasure and horror struck at once. She wanted to see him. But she was still wearing her sweat suit, her hair was hooked behind her ears and she hadn't put on any makeup today.

"Gracie?" he called through the door.

She made a face but after some quick mental calculations realized there was no way to get upstairs, put on better clothes, comb her hair and slap on some mascara before he saw her. Giving in to the unavoidable, she finally hollered to him, "Come on in, it's open." Then, when she heard him close the front door after himself, she said, "I'm in the kitchen. I have one more platter to put away and I'm finished."

She set the dish on a shelf above the refrigerator, closed the cupboard and headed for the chair she'd used as a stepladder at the other end of the counter.

"What are you doing?" he asked in part amusement, part disbelief as he watched her do a tightrope walk across the front edge of the kitchen sink.

"Cleaning cupboards to sort out what of Adeline's I can store to make room for my own things," she explained as she reached the end of the counter and her waiting chair. If only there was a graceful way to step down onto it. But the seat was too low to allow for grace. She had to turn her back to Gabe, grab one of the cupboard handles and jut her butt out into space to get down. She felt like an idiot.

"Here, let me help you."

His hands came around her waist, one of them against her bare skin where her sweatshirt had pulled up. Did he have the hottest hands in the world or was there just that much heat generated by his touch? It must have been heat generated by his touch because by the time her feet were back on the floor her whole body felt flushed.

"Thanks," she said, hoping her face wasn't as red as it felt and wondering if his hands had been a little slow in leaving her waist or if she was imagining it.

"Isn't it late to be cleaning cupboards?"

She unhooked her hair from behind her ears and glanced up at him, finding him smiling as if he hadn't even noticed how she looked. It made her feel better. "I've been at this all day. But it's finally done."

"Great, then you can offer me a cup of that coffee over there." He nodded toward the pot that was half-full. "There's something I need to talk to you about."

"I turned the coffeemaker off a little while ago. All right if I heat a couple of cups in the microwave?"

"Works for me."

Gabe crossed his arms over his plaid shirt and leaned his jeans-clad hips back against the counter right next to her as Gracie filled two mugs, set them in the single modern appliance in the room, and turned it on.

A split second later the whole house went pitch-black.

"Oh-oh, what did I do wrong?" she said.

"You blew a fuse."

"But I've used the microwave twice today and this didn't happen."

"I'll bet you didn't have lights on before, did you?"

"Nope, I didn't," she confirmed. "Now what?"

"Give me your hand," he ordered, finding it with amazingly accurate aim when she reached out and missed. "I'll show you where the flashlight is and teach you how to change a fuse."

His hand around hers wasn't abnormally warm, but it was big and firm with a texture like kidskin—tough but smooth and uncallused—and it imparted to her that same sense of heat as when he'd helped her down moments before.

He led the way through the kitchen and into the laundry room without incident. "Unless you moved it, the flashlight should be on the shelf with the detergents."

He still held her hand though there was no need and Gracie was enjoying the sensation too much to be the one to let go. Then she heard him exclaim over having found the flashlight and he had to release her hand to turn it on. She was instantly sorry to lose his touch.

"There," he said as a beam of light flooded the small room. Gabe took a fuse from the jar that held them and demonstrated how to replace the old with the new. Gracie only hoped she would know how to do it when the need arose again because her mind was more on the sensations running through her in response to him than on what he was teaching her.

With the fuse changed, Gabe went around turning off all the lights except one small lamp over the kitchen table while Gracie reset the clock-timer on the microwave.

"Okay, try again," Gabe told her. This time heating the coffee went off without a hitch.

They took their cups to the table and sat down across from one another. Gracie sipped her coffee, glancing at Gabe as she did, to find him grinning at her.

"You know, in my much newer house across the street I can run the microwave *and* have lights on at the same time. And if I overload a circuit all I have to do is switch the breaker back on."

"Yes, but does your much newer house across the street have a kitchen floor that creaks?"

"Why would I want a kitchen floor that creaks?"

"Because it has such a homey sound."

He laughed. "No doubt about it, you are as strange as your aunt. I suppose you even like that old midget refrigerator." He nodded in the direction of the antiquated appliance her aunt had called an icebox.

Gracie wrinkled her nose. "No, I have to admit I'm not crazy about that or the stove that threatens to singe my eyebrows every time I use it."

"You mean they aren't part of the hominess of this place?" He pretended to be shocked.

"I like the conveniences of modern machinery as much as the next person. In fact, I've been wondering all day long what my aunt would say to my replacing them."

"She'd say go ahead—the truth is I was about to take her appliance shopping when she left. She was tired of having her milk spoil because the fridge doesn't work right anymore, and the stove *did* singe her eyebrows not long ago." One side of his mouth tilted up in a devilish smile. "Be nice to me and I might consider getting you the same deal I was going to get your aunt."

"What do you mean be nice to you? I already gave you reheated coffee. How much nicer can I get?"

He wiggled his bushy eyebrows up and down, and lowered his eyelids in an exaggeratedly lascivious expression. "You will have to be much, much nicer."

"Adeline didn't tell me you were a lecher."

"I hid my true colors from her. She'd have taken me up on it."

"And you don't think I will."

"One can only hope."

They both laughed and Gracie felt pretty pleased with herself for holding her own in her first full-blown flirting attempt.

Gabe took a drink of coffee. "Seriously, I have a good friend who owns an appliance store. He gives me a discount because I give him so much business, moving the way I do."

"Moving the way you do?"

"A lot. I've been in the house across the street the longest I've ever lived anywhere—three years."

"You can't be serious?" she said, showing her horror of the idea. "Why do you move so much?"

"I like the change," he explained simply. "I like to clear the slate—so to speak. I toss out everything I've accumulated that isn't absolutely necessary, move to a new place and start over fresh."

"I'd hate that! I have to have continuity and roots."

He glanced around the room. "Well, you're certainly in pretty deep here."

"Which is where I intend to stay until I die and leave this house to someone else who will appreciate it."

"Well, then, you'd better get new appliances because what's here now will never make it into the next generation. How about tomorrow night? I know I can arrange with my friend for you to pick out whatever you want then."

Gracie took him up on the offer. Then she said, "Didn't you say you had something you wanted to talk to me about?"

That sobered him up considerably. She watched his brows draw together as he stared at his cup for a moment.

"I didn't want us to have to get into this right off the bat—that's why I haven't brought it up. But I'm afraid it can't wait. We need to finalize the deal on the comics."

Now it was Gracie's turn to frown. "You've lost me."

"The Baby Jack Flash comic books—the sale Adeline and I were in the middle of arranging to the collectors I represent," he said as if to prompt her memory.

Gracie shook her head. "I don't know what you're talking about. Is that what you do for a living—sell comic books?"

Gabe studied her for a moment. "You honestly don't know?"

Gracie shrugged. "I don't know what you do for a living, no. And as for comic books—I didn't know Adeline had any."

"She doesn't. You do. They're part of what you inherited from her," Gabe said, still watching her as if to read something on her face. "You didn't get a letter from your aunt recently?"

"She left a note that introduced you and said you'd acquaint me with the workings of the house."

"No, this would have come before. She sent it to you in Australia."

"I had a letter from her in June that she'd written early in May—sometimes my mail came without any problems and other times I'd get letters a long time after they were sent."

"The letter I'm talking about was written the first of this month."

Gracie shook her head. "I didn't get anything from her after the May letter."

Gabe grimaced. "You can't mean that," he groaned.

"Maybe you ought to explain this to me from the beginning."

"I own a shop called The Collector's Exchange—do you know about that?"

She shrugged. "Sorry."

Gabe explained the shop and his financial problems. "I didn't even know Adeline had any comic books until one night two months ago when she caught me after a particularly bad day. She kept after me about why I was in such a rotten mood and finally I confided the money troubles to her. That was when she told me about three comic books she'd bought in 1938—Baby Jack Flash."

"In 1938 Adeline would have been in her twenties—why would she have bought comic books?"

"Baby Jack Flash was one of the first to come out with original material in magazine form—before that, comic books were only reprints of strips run in newspapers. Adeline bought the first three of Baby Jack Flash because they were a novelty that caught her fancy. And Adeline, being Adeline, never threw them away."

That made sense to Gracie. Adeline had always shown a childlike interest in things—somewhere in the attic Gracie had no doubt there was still a rock collection, boxes of seashells, the first Kewpie doll that had ever caught Adeline's attention and, of course, there were the soap dishes from around the world.

Gabe went on. "Adeline offered the comics to me that night. It was like finding a gold mine, and I'd just made contact with this group of collectors who I thought would be interested in original issues of Baby Jack Flash. The details would only bore you, but they were definitely interested, and I was negotiating the sale. We had tentatively reached an agreement of sixty thousand dollars for the three."

"Sixty thousand dollars for comic books?" she repeated, astounded by the amount.

Gabe nodded. "Anyway, before we could finalize the deal Adeline got the call about her acceptance to the monastery." Gabe explained why the sale didn't go through. "But she sent you a letter telling you all of this, including that you were to finish the transaction when you got here."

Gracie raised both of her hands a few inches from around her mug. "I didn't get the letter."

Gabe was obviously unhappy to hear that but he forged on, anyway. "Well, even without it we can go ahead with the sale—you own everything free and clear. And my clients are getting antsy about the delay. That's why I came tonight even though I'd wanted to wait until you were settled in."

Gracie didn't say anything for a moment, feeling very much put on the spot. Then, carefully, she said, "You do know that the reason my aunt left me her things was because she knew I *wouldn't* sell anything, don't you?"

"Yes, that was why she sent you the letter—to assure you that selling the comics was what she wanted in this case."

"But I didn't get the letter," she reminded him.

"And Adeline can't be reached, so without the letter you don't have anything but my word on it that that's what she wanted you to do," he finished for her.

"It isn't that I think you're lying," Gracie added quickly, though she hadn't forgotten how strongly her aunt felt about what Adeline called reducing her belongings to cash value. "But I didn't even know she had these comic books. If she wanted you to sell them that's fine with me. It's just that to do it without knowing for sure that that was what she intended makes me really uncomfortable."

That didn't seem to disturb him. He nodded. "I understand, Gracie. I asked her not to tell my father about our arrangement because at the time he didn't know the shop was in trouble and I didn't want him to worry about it. but I'm sure your aunt told somebody else what she had in mind. Will you ask around for me?"

It was such a relief that he was taking it this way. Gracie smiled. "Of course, I will."

"And when you have some confirmation we can go through with the sale?"

"Sure."

He smiled at her again, the worry lines erased from his face, and Gracie felt that warmth again even without being touched by him.

Then he reached across the table and took her hand, squeezing it gently. "Thanks. This is really a big deal for me, and I'd like to get it taken care of as soon as possible. I'll also be glad when we can put it behind us and just concentrate on getting to know each other."

Those smoky blue eyes of his held hers as surely as his fingers wrapped around her hand, and she was willingly lost in them. "I'd like that," she heard herself say before she even realized she was going to.

His smile broadened into a grin as if her wanting to get to know him better was more important to him than the comic books. Then he tightened his hold on her hand. "I'd better get home. Murf has been alone there for a long time and I imagine you're tired after a whole day of cabinet climbing."

She wanted to say that she couldn't imagine ever being too tired to want to sit with him in the cozy confines of the kitchen, looking into that handsome face, into those extraordinary eyes, hearing the deep, dark honey of his voice waft around her. But of course, that would have been crazy. Instead they both stood and went to the front door where he turned to face her, looking down at her with a Cheshire-cat smile.

"Tomorrow night for appliance shopping, then, right?"

He was standing so close in front of her that she had to tip her head back to look at him and somehow he had hold of her hand again. "Right. If you don't mind."

"I have an appointment early in the evening, so how about seven-thirty?"

"Fine."

He smiled at her, his thumb making small, feather-light circles against the back of her hand, his eyes holding hers. But he made no move to leave.

And Gracie wasn't anxious for him to. The air between them seemed charged, and just when she was wondering if he really was going to kiss her tonight his face came slowly nearer, as if giving her plenty of time to back away if she wanted to.

But she didn't want to, and that was the only thought in her head at that moment.

His mouth finally met hers, softly at first, his lips barely parted. And then, when Gracie arched her neck back a little farther to meet him, he deepened the kiss.

She could feel his breath on her cheek, hot but not as hot as what was coursing through her in response to the velvet feel of his mouth over hers. He smelled faintly of after-shave, and the only other part of their bodies that touched were their hands, where he held hers firmly in his.

And then, almost before it began, the kiss ended. Gracie opened her eyes to find him smiling down at her again.

"Good night," he said, his voice a little raspy and barely above a whisper.

"See you tomorrow." She stood right where she was as he opened the door, then the screen, holding it while he gave her one last glance and pulled the door closed between them. And she kept on standing there, watching as he took care to replace the screen and left.

That was when she caught sight of herself—old sweat suit, hair hooked behind her ears again even though she didn't remember doing it, looking the worse for wear.

But all she could do was laugh at herself. She felt too terrific to care.

Chapter Four

"Come on, Murf, you lazy thing," Gabe called to his dog as he held the front door open early the next morning.

Eli was waiting at the curb for their walk, laughing at the big Saint Bernard as he lumbered out in his own good time.

When Gabe and Murf finally joined his father, Gabe looked the older man up and down. "You're dressed pretty snazzy today," he commented as they set off at a fast pace down the street.

Eli wore a new gray-and-maroon sweat suit, and his sparse white hair was combed as neatly as if he was going to brunch instead. He cast a glance at Gabe's cutoffs and tank top. "There isn't anything wrong with looking nice, is there?"

"You usually wear that old blue jumpsuit thing."

But Eli didn't answer him. Instead, he was grinning ear to ear as they turned the corner and came upon the older woman they saw most mornings sitting on a side porch having her coffee.

Eli waved and called hello. Then, still smiling, he said in a confidential aside, "Her name is Marge. I've had my eye on her, and last night we met at the grocery store. In produce. She was squeezing avocados. Hardly an age spot on her."

Gabe laughed. "Don't tell me you have her in your sights for wife number seven."

"You never know. I've been alone a long time. I don't like it."

"You've only been divorced a year."

"A year is a long time. I could have a stroke tomorrow. You wouldn't want to have to hold my dribble cloth, would you?"

"Oh, no, you should definitely have a wife for that," Gabe said facetiously, laughing. "Do me a favor, will you? Don't rush into another marriage. Get to know the woman, let her get to know you. Think long and hard, and take a good look at everything from all different angles before you jump in again."

"I know by that advice that you've never been in real love," Eli said sagely.

Gabe rolled his eyes. "Maybe if you ever waited to see if you were in real love before doing a spring to the altar, you would not have so many divorces under your belt."

"That isn't how it happens, Gabe. You meet a woman, you can't stop thinking about her, you dream about her, your mind wanders to her even when you're trying not to think about her, you can't wait to see her, you don't want to leave her when you do...." Eli sighed. "All of those rational things you're wanting me to do are just not possible."

Ordinarily Gabe would have argued that. He'd have said what his father was talking about might be true of adolescents but it shouldn't be true of grown men.

But this time, instead of what his father had said sounding like romantic drivel to Gabe, it was as if Eli had described symptoms that Gabe was experiencing firsthand.

And that gave him pause.

"You better get Murf out of the street." Eli's voice broke into Gabe's reverie in time for him to see that the dog had wandered off the sidewalk.

"I still think you can keep your feelings under control enough to exercise a little good judgment," he told his father finally, needing to believe it was true.

Eli chuckled knowingly. "Nice theory, but feelings tend to have a will of their own. Sometimes there's just no keeping control over them, son. Wait and see, wait and see."

The wait could be over, Gabe thought, surprised at himself, and slightly unnerved.

They walked a few more steps before the older man said, "So, how are things going with your Gracie?"

Was there a sly note to his father's voice? "I'm taking her to buy new appliances tonight," he answered in what seemed like safe territory.

"How did that come about?"

"I had to go over to her place last night to talk to her and it just came up that she wanted to replace Adeline's old relics. I offered to get her the discount Scott Shimel gives me."

"So you saw her again last night. Seems like you can't stay away."

"I couldn't last night. I had a call from one of the members of that group of collectors who want the Baby Jack Flash comics—Simonesque."

That changed the subject immediately. Eli sobered. "Simonesque is the lawyer you don't like, isn't he? What did he want?"

"He said the group is unhappy with the delay. But from the tone of the call, he, at least, sounds more than unhappy. I decided I couldn't wait any longer to talk to Gracie."

"And?"

Gabe blew out a sorry-sounding breath. "And she never got Adeline's letter and didn't have the foggiest idea what I was talking about."

"That doesn't sound good."

"It isn't great, that's for sure. The letter would have explained the whole thing to Gracie and we probably could have finished the deal last night. As it is she needs some time to ask around and find out if anybody knows about our arrangement."

"Because of the stipulation that she not sell or get rid of anything," Eli guessed.

"On the nose."

"I told Adeline that was a silly thing to impose on her niece. I said, how could she expect that girl to take over her house, lock, stock and barrel, and not throw some things out or sell some of it? But would Addie listen to me? No sirree. She said she hadn't kept all the things that meant something to her all these years just to have somebody go through and trash it or sell it. And besides, she claimed, Gracie was a pack rat, too. She'd understand. Well, if she's a pack rat, I said, how is she going to get all of her own things in there with all of yours—"

Gabe had to jump in. He knew that when his father went off on one of these tangents he was likely to relate several hours' worth of he-said-she-said conversation before he was through. "The point is that Adeline did make her wishes clear and Gracie takes them very seriously."

"I just hope my Addie didn't change her mind about selling those comics to you and that's why Gracie never received the letter."

"Adeline didn't change her mind."

They left the park that marked the end of their second mile and headed back for Gabe's house. For a block they didn't say anything, both of them watching Murf as he sniffed fire hydrants and light poles.

When Eli spoke again it was tentatively, as if he were treading on thin ice. "You know, I have a little money saved—"

That was as far as he got. "And you'd better keep it saved."

"I could keep part of it saved and use the rest as an investment in The Collector's Exchange."

"I hear dribble cloths are pretty expensive. And we know how expensive it is to marry women to hold them."

"I'd like to help you out," Eli insisted, ignoring Gabe's joke.

"Thanks, Pop, but no. I'll close my doors before I'll take your savings. Besides, what The Collector's Exchange needs—what those comics will give it—is more than a financial bailout. It needs a boost into the future. And anyway, if this deal falls through and it looks like I've led these buyers on, no amount of money will be able to fix the damage an impression like that will do to my reputation."

"I hadn't thought about that."

Gabe glanced at his father, seeing the worry lines in his already creased face. He regretted that Eli knew any of what was going on. "There won't be a problem. Somebody is bound to know about this arrangement with Adeline, and as soon as Gracie confirms it, we'll go right into the sale."

Eli was quiet for a moment. Then he said, "What if Adeline didn't tell anybody about your deal? She was better at keeping secrets than anyone I ever knew and if she thought you didn't want people to know about your problems—well, she just might have kept it to herself all the way around. What happens then?"

"I don't know. Gracie and I didn't talk about that."

And Gabe didn't even want to think about it.

"Comic books, comic books, where are the comic books?" Gracie chanted to herself as she stood in the middle of the attic, wondering where to start looking. Obviously they'd been taken out recently, but she hadn't found them in any of the rest of the house, so Adeline must have put them back in the attic.

The most logical place, Gracie thought, was on the shelves with the books along the only wall whose contents she had really looked at. But she didn't find them there, or anywhere else among what lined that space.

"Next," she said, turning to scan the second wall. A rolltop desk, two old bureaus and a sideboard faced her. She lifted the rolltop, opened all the drawers on the bureau and the doors on the sideboard, but while she found an assortment of odds and ends, there were no comic books.

The third wall held lamps, knickknacks, paintings, clocks, crockery and boxes and boxes of clothes and shoes—some of which dated back to the turn of the century.

Gracie was reasonably sure her aunt hadn't tucked valuable old magazines in with the clothes, and since Willy was due to pick her up soon she decided to bypass them. Instead, she turned to the last section of the attic, the one farthest to the back where she had to bend over to keep from hitting her head on the sloped ceiling.

The first thing she came to was an antique tricycle—three iron wheels attached to a carved wooden horse, the handlebars rising up from the animal's head. The paint was chipped and faded. But looking beyond time's havoc, Gracie could see what a beautiful old beast it was. She itched to restore it to its original state, and promised herself that as soon as she could get the two households blended together and free her saws, tools and supplies, that was just what she'd do.

But the tricycle was only the beginning of the toys that occupied this portion of the attic. As kids, Gracie, Willy and Dean had wrinkled their noses at Adeline's suggestions that they play with what had been their aunt's childhood entertainments. Rag dolls instead of Barbies? Wooden tops instead of Frisbees? Music boxes rather than records? Hand-carved puzzles instead of jigsaws?

But seeing it all now, Gracie had a new appreciation for it. The toys had a quiet beauty all their own. If she had a child, she thought, she'd use them to decorate the nursery.

If she had a child.

She and Burt had been infertile. They'd suffered through all the tests and procedures only to find no answer at all. They were both perfectly healthy and capable of conceiving. But somehow it had never happened.

Would that be different with another man? she wondered.

And then a split second later she realized what had crossed her mind. Thoughts of having a baby with a man other than Burt? Oh, she felt guilty for that, almost as if his death had opened the way to a new opportunity for her.

But it wasn't that at all, she insisted to herself. She'd accepted that she might never have children. She could have lived a full, happy life without them, just she and Burt alone. There had been other options had they been that determined to become parents. But they'd agreed to just let nature take its course.

And yet, a little flutter of hope crept back into her heart. Acceptance hadn't changed the fact that she'd always wanted a baby. It had only boxed up the desire and put it away like those old clothes. And suddenly the box was open again, right beside the image of Gabe in her mind.

"One kiss and you're putting him and babies in the same thought?" she asked herself.

Well, it had been a pretty good kiss. But enjoying the feelings he was bringing alive in her was one thing. Taking it so far as to put him and the idea of a baby together was something else again.

"Get back to business," she ordered resolutely.

There was no sign of the comic books anywhere among the toys, and all that was left to be searched was an old cedar chest shoved into the corner. The last hope.

She moved a stack of blankets and quilts from the top of the chest, and got down on her knees in front of it. The hinges on the lid squeaked as she lifted it. Inside she found a porcelain piggy bank that still had coins in it—if the sound it made when she lifted it out didn't lie. Underneath were doll clothes and blankets—shapeless buntings and hand-crocheted rectangles, all in smaller versions of the real things.

Gracie took the doll clothes out and set them on top of the quilts. What was left in the trunk were two wooden marionettes and the tea set from which Adeline's sachet dishes had originated. But under all of that was a smaller cedar box the size of a shirt box. Gracie took it out and opened it.

The comics were inside. Three crisp magazines that looked as if they'd never been read. Gracie glanced through them. The first copy introduced Baby Jack Flash. Petal pink and chubby, the diapered baby sported a single spiked curl of blond hair.

The stories in all three seemed to follow the same formula—Baby Jack Flash crawled away from his mother into one perilous adventure after another, rescued on the brink of destruction by the ever-vigilant mutt, Sam, who received a loving scolding at the end from the mother, who believed the dog had led the baby astray.

The stories were naive, but the artwork was finely detailed, the colors still rich.

Satisfied that she knew where the magazines were now, she put them back in the cedar box, still amazed by how much money they were worth.

For years her brother, Dean, had been saying that Adeline was sitting on a gold mine here. Little did he know.

Gracie replaced the box in the trunk and set everything else on top of it just the way they had been before. Then she closed the lid and stacked the quilts again, feeling confident the comics would be safe there for a few more days until she could sell them to Gabe's clients.

Just as she finished she caught the faint ring of the telephone and made a dash down the attic steps to her room.

"Hello?" she answered.

"You sound out of breath."

"Dean!" she said, recognizing her brother's voice instantly. "I was just thinking about you. Are you finally home?"

"As of this morning. I got your message on my machine and here I am, returning your call. How's tricks?"

"Tricks are great. But I have to ask you something."

"Save it for tonight and I'll take you to dinner. I'm dying to show you the Shaker table I just got. It needs a little work but nothing you can't handle."

"I can't tonight. Gabe is taking me to buy new appliances."

"Gabe?"

The tone of Dean's voice made Gracie laugh. She'd heard it all too often growing up—it was his protective big-brother voice. "Gabe Duran, Eli Duran's son and Adeline's neighbor? The man who she enlisted to teach me how to run things around here? He's been a big help. But anyway," she rushed on, changing the subject, "what I have to ask you can't wait." Gracie explained Gabe's interest in the comics and her dilemma.

"Our Adeline was actually selling something?" he said once she'd finished. "I find that hard to believe."

Gracie knew this was going to happen. She knew her brother was going to get his nose bent out of joint the minute he found out Adeline had agreed to sell anything to *anyone*. In fact, she'd been steadfastly against letting Dean's antique store handle even things in the attic that she no longer had any use for.

"I take it your finding it hard to believe that she'd sell something means you don't know anything about an agreement between Gabe and Adeline," Gracie said.

"I'm the last person on the face of the earth to whom our aunt would have confided such a thing. Especially after all those lectures I had to sit through about my callously wanting to sell off her memories for mere money."

"You dished out your own fair share trying to get her to let you add half her household to your inventory."

"I'd have made us both good profits."

"And instead she left you all her cash. Ample compensation, wasn't it?"

"The old girl always was generous to a fault. I guess she made sure we both got what we wanted, but I have to admit, I still would have dearly loved to get my hands on some of those antiques," he said with an affectionate laugh. Then, "Have I understood you right? The only thing that verifies the fact that there was an agreement to sell these comic books at all is some letter you never got?"

"Right?"

"I don't like it," Dean said ominously. "You realize, of course, that it's possible this neighbor could only be claiming there was a letter and an agreement—it could be a ploy to get his hands on something that Adeline refused to sell him just the way she refused to sell everything else."

"Or he could just be telling the truth." Gracie didn't understand it, but the inclination to defend Gabe was strong.

"Well, I don't like it," Dean repeated. "And is this guy buttering you up, too?"

"He's being neighborly and friendly." Okay, so that kiss had gone beyond both, but she realized from many teenage years of experience that to let Dean know Gabe had kissed her would be a mistake.

"You know, Gracie, you're very vulnerable right now," he said, apparently guessing at what she wasn't saying.

"He's a nice man, Dean. He's also the son of a very old friend of Adeline's and a friend of hers in his own right."

"Which is how he could have gotten to know she had these comics in the first place. But she wouldn't even let me sell her precious belongings and I'm her own flesh and blood. Keep that in mind."

"I haven't agreed to anything but asking around to learn if Gabe's claim can be confirmed."

"Well, I'm glad to hear that, at least. And if this Gabe character makes a pass at you, you just let me know."

Gracie rolled her eyes. Dean was barely five foot seven, and weighed a hundred and thirty pounds sopping wet. He was no match for Gabe. "I can take care of myself, but thanks for the offer."

"I'm serious, Gracie. I know you must be lonely and a new man looks like a quick fix, but—"

"I'm not lonely." Not anymore, at least. "I'm here with you and Willy now, and Mom and Dad will be back before long."

"Still, we can't take the place of a husband."

True enough. "I'm okay and I'm not going to do anything rash in the romance department. Okay?"

"Rash in the romance department? Sounds like a euphemism for a social disease," he said with a laugh. "Anyway, think you can squeeze me in for a visit tomorrow sometime?"

"As far as I know I'll be here all day. Come over whenever you can."

Gracie hung up and checked the clock. Willy was due to pick her up in five minutes for lunch. There wasn't time to do more than run a brush through her hair before her cousin pulled up in her van and honked.

Gracie locked the house and went out. They weren't even at the end of the block before she'd explained what was happening with the comic books, asking Willy if Adeline had confided anything to her.

"This is the first I've heard of it, but I think it's great. Sell the dusty old things. Surely getting rid of a little would be okay."

Gracie wasn't surprised by the response. Though she was getting tired of pointing it out, she repeated that to sell the magazines without knowing for sure if that was Adeline's intention would be breaking a trust.

"Personally," Willy said, "I've thought it was crummy that Dean and I inherited so much actual cash and what can immediately be converted to actual cash while all Adeline left you was a houseful of relics hung up in a condition that ties your hands. I feel as if Dean and I won the lottery and you got the booby prize. At least if you sell the comics you come out with a fat consolation."

"I don't need a consolation. I'm thrilled to have what she left me," Gracie assured her cousin. "I just don't want to sell anything that she didn't mean for me to. So, will you ask around, see if any of the family knows about this arrangement with Gabe? If I call, everyone will have to be brought up to date and it'll take me forever. If you call you can get right to the point and hang up."

Willy wrinkled her nose in answer.

"Come on," Gracie cajoled. "While you do that I'm going to go through Adeline's address book and call all of her friends to ask the same thing."

"Yuk, I'd hate to do that even more than calling all the relatives."

"Does that mean you'll help me out, then?"

"I shouldn't do anything to help Gabe Duran since he never looked twice at me. But damn his blue eyes, I guess I will."

"Thanks," Gracie said, left with a vivid image of those blue eyes Willy had just brought to mind once again.

Buying a new tan-colored jumpsuit with full sleeves and a high, tight-fitting collar to go shopping for appliances was crazy, but Gracie had done it, anyway. And in preparation for the evening she had luxuriated in a hot bubble bath, powdered and perfumed herself to within an inch of her life, washed and conditioned her hair, and applied her usual light makeup with as much care as on her wedding day. She was looking forward to her seven-thirty date with Gabe. To say the least.

But at eight o'clock she was still waiting for him.

By eight-fifteen she began to wonder if she was being stood up.

That was when the phone rang.

"There's nothing I hate more than someone being late," Gabe said in answer to her hello.

"Me, too," she responded, but without rancor. Just the sound of his deep, rich voice sent her stomach fluttering and dissolved any peevishness she might have felt.

"I'm really sorry. I was sure I'd be home long before now. Luckily the appliance store is in the middle of a midnight madness sale so we still have plenty of time. Unless you never want to see my ugly mug again."

Not likely. "I'll forgive you this time."

"And you won't be sorry," he said with a teasingly lascivious tone to his voice. "So, tell me, if you're all ready—which I assume you are—would you mind coming over to keep me company while I take care of Murf before we go?''

"I think I can probably handle that."

"Terrific. The front door is open, so just come in."

Ten minutes later Gracie found Gabe in his kitchen spooning carrots, broccoli, cauliflower, potatoes and rice into a big ceramic dish.

"Doggy stew," Gabe informed her. "Murf can't tolerate dog food anymore now that he's in his golden years, so I cook this up for him."

"It smells good enough for human consumption."

"It is. If I'm really pressed for time I heat some for myself, too. But then I have to hide to eat it or Murf gives me a look that says he thinks I've taken the food out of his mouth."

While Gabe finished fixing the gourmet dog meal, Gracie told him that she'd asked Willy and Dean about the comics and that neither of them had known anything. "But I have Willy checking with all the relatives so I can just contact Adeline's friends to see if anyone knows anything," she explained.

"Great, thanks. I appreciate it," he said. Then as he set the bowl on the floor in front of the stoically waiting animal, he changed the subject. "Any chance I could persuade you to let me take a quick shower before we go?"

He didn't look as if he needed one and Gracie wondered if he just wanted to spruce up for her the way she had for him. It was a thought that made all of her own ministrations worth it. "Since the store will be open so late anyway, I don't mind waiting."

"I'll only be a few minutes," he assured her, squeezing her arm as he walked around her. "Make yourself comfortable—turn on the TV if you want."

But Gracie wasn't in the mood for television. The last time she'd been here, the morning after she'd arrived, she'd had eyes only for Gabe, so she hadn't really noticed anything about the house itself. Now she took the opportunity to look around a little.

As she went from the kitchen into the dining room she realized for the first time just how sparsely decorated the place was. Nothing but an all-white kitchen set took up the space that could easily have accommodated a full dining table and chairs as well as a china hutch and sideboard.

From there she walked into the living room that was actually just the other end of one long, open section. It was equally devoid of knickknacks or frills. There were no pictures on the walls, and not so much as an ashtray on the end tables.

Against one wall was a high-tech television, VCR and stereo system, with the TV and the VCR placed on the speakers. The plain, functional modern furniture consisted of a black couch and a white chair at right angles to one another, with a boxlike coffee table set in front of both—close enough so that feet could be put up from either. There were two lamps that looked like spaceships and a wall clock propped on the floor.

"I know you have to hate my taste," Gabe said from behind her.

"I feel like I've landed in a future century," she answered tactfully. Then she turned to look at him for the first time.

His hair was shiny wet but combed more smoothly than she had ever seen it before. He was freshly shaven and smelled of the woodsy scent she remembered from the first night she'd met him. He wore a pair of khaki slacks that fit his hips without an inch to spare and a hunter green rugby shirt with long sleeves.

Gracie watched him curve his big, long-fingered hand around his opposite wrist and slide the sleeve to his elbow. In her mind she could feel that same hand, warm and tough skinned, trailing a slow path up her own arm. The sensation was so vivid that goose bumps erupted there.

Belatedly, she realized he was saying something.

"I know how you must feel here. Every time I step into your place it seems like I should be dressed in a swallow-tailed coat and a wing collar."

He'd probably look good in that, too, she thought. But instead she said, "Shall we go?"

"I'm all set," he agreed, taking her elbow.

There was something about his touch that made her want to melt into him and she fought the urge as he guided her through a door that stood between the dining room and living room, leading into the garage.

Gracie had seen Gabe's car several times as he came and went, but she had never seen the newer model parked beside it in the double garage.

"This is the reason I was late tonight. I had to close the deal on this car and it took longer than it should have," he said as he held the door open on the smart-looking black sports coupe.

"You bought a new car?" she said, surprised and unable to keep herself from wondering why he would invest in something like that when his other car was nearly new and at a time when he claimed he was having financial difficulties so severe Adeline had agreed to help him out.

As if he read her mind, he explained when he got behind the wheel and began to back out. "I lease my cars and the lease on the old one is up this week. It was cheaper for me to take out a new lease on this than try to get a loan on the other one. And there's nothing quite like a new car. Don't you love the smell?"

"Mmm, it's nice," she agreed, chastising herself for her negative thoughts of a moment before and deciding she'd allowed her brother's cynicism to influence her more than she realized.

Gabe started the engine and then had to search for reverse to back out of the garage. "That's the trouble with a new car—you don't know what you're doing at first."

"And you have to break it in."

"You say that as if it's a hardship. I love to break in a new car," he told her as he headed for the highway. Then he glanced over at her and laughed. "Don't tell me, you like ancient jalopies, too."

"I beg your pardon. My car is not a jalopy. But it is six years old and I'm sort of attached to it. It's taken me this long to feel comfortable with it and to get to know all its quirks."

"When cars start getting quirky it's time to get something reliable. You believe in doing it with kitchen appliances but not with a piece of machinery that could leave you stranded on a dark, deserted road?"

"I'm never going to live down getting new appliances, am I?" she teased.

"Never."

"So I have a little chink in my armor. You do, too," she goaded.

"I most certainly do not."

"I saw you leave your house to walk with your father this morning and you were wearing the oldest pair of cutoffs and tank top I've ever seen in my life. Those things are so ancient you couldn't give them away."

He laughed. "Okay, you caught me," he conceded. "I'm surprised you missed the tennis shoes—they're godawful gray and one of them even has a hole in the toe."

"But you love them."

"I have to admit that nothing feels quite as good that early in the morning."

And Gracie had to admit that she'd enjoyed the sight. His big, broad shoulders had been bare, the scoop of the neck had shown the slight shadow of hair on his chest, the muscles of his biceps had been exposed and there had been a hole in the tank top that had given a hint of the ridges of his flat stomach.

But he was talking again, pointing out a house he'd lived in before the one across the street from Adeline's. Gracie tried to whip her wandering thoughts into shape to listen but it wasn't easy, and for the remainder of the ride to the appliance store she fought the battle as he narrated a tour that covered three apartments and two more houses he'd lived in before.

Shopping for a refrigerator, stove and dishwasher hardly made for an exciting evening, and yet when the chore was accomplished Gracie had to admit it had been a long time since she'd enjoyed anything quite as much. And Gabe got all the credit. His sense of humor kept everything light and left her feeling more relaxed and free to be herself than she had with anyone but Burt. Had this been a fancy date she couldn't have had more fun.

As Gabe pulled back into his garage Gracie tried to think of a way to prolong the evening. It took her until he was walking her across the street before she thought of something. "I went through Adeline's photograph albums this morning and kept out all the ones with snap-shots of her and your father. Why don't you come in for coffee and you can take a look at them and pick some you think he'd like to have?''

"Today was one of those days when I drank enough coffee to float, and if you don't mind, I think it would be better if my father chose what pictures he'd like to have," he said.

Gracie's spirits sank.

Then he went on, "But I'd love to see the snapshots myself and then I could take the albums with me so my father could look through them. "How would that be?''

It wasn't easy for her to keep her smile from being too big. "That would be fine," she answered as she un-locked her front door and led the way in.

All the photographs involving Eli were in four albums that held snapshots of no one but the two old friends. Gracie had left all four on the coffee table in the living room, where she'd sat with her lemon water and glanced through them before heading for the attic this morning.

She turned on the two Tiffany lamps on either side of the sofa. "I forgot it before, but when I was out with Willy today I bought a bottle of wine. Could I tempt you with a glass of that?''

"Perfect. It'll counteract all the caffeine running through me from the coffee.''

"Why don't you start looking through the albums while I get it?'' she suggested, leaving him alone in the living room. A few minutes later she was back with two glasses of white wine.

Gabe patted the plush velvet cushion next to him in invitation. "Go through these with me in case there are some you don't want to part with.''

That was as good a reason as any Gracie could think of to share the couch with him. The light through the stained glass of the lamps lent a rosy hue to the room. When she sat down Gabe moved nearer and completed the feeling of cozy intimacy.

"They made a pretty cute couple, I have to say that for them," Gabe said as he set the album half on her lap and half on his so she could see, too.

"They were, weren't they?" Gracie responded, though in truth she was thinking less about her aunt and Eli Duran than about the feel of Gabe's thigh running the length of her own.

She took a sip of her wine and set the glass on the coffee table beside Gabe's, trying to concentrate on the pictures again. But somehow her gaze settled on his thumb instead. His nail was cut short and neat. Then she let her eyes trail it past his big knuckle on up to his wrist—thick and shaded with a smattering of coarse hair.

From there she ran a slow visual path up the corded tendons of his forearms, wishing her hand could travel it instead and feel the texture of his skin before it disappeared inside the pushed-up sleeve of his shirt.

Gracie took a bigger drink of her wine and tried to get some control over herself.

"Would you look at that?" Gabe was saying. "That's the two of them on the elephant at the zoo. How do you suppose they managed to get up there with the kids?"

"Nothing was beyond my aunt," Gracie managed to answer, wishing afterward that her voice hadn't come out so huskily.

And then those dangerously independent eyes of hers went from the bottom photograph on the album page to Gabe's nearby lap. She nearly broke out into a sweat before jerking her gaze back to the photographs on the page he turned just then.

"Too bad things never worked out for them," she said in a rush, the first thing to come to mind as she looked at a picture of Adeline and Eli hugging under a sprig of mistletoe.

Gabe was a little slow in responding and when Gracie glanced at his face she found him looking at her instead of at the pictures. It took him another moment to turn back to them and respond to what she'd said about her aunt and his father. "Maybe if they'd gotten together earlier it would have saved my father all those divorces. I could be wrong, but I think he would have stayed with Adeline."

His voice was as deep and ragged as Gracie's had been and she knew from the sound of it that his thoughts weren't completely on those old pictures, either.

Then, in a tone that was much more intimate than before, he said, "What about you, Gracie? Did you like being married?"

"Yes, I did. I guess it was just dumb luck, though, since the wedding was two weeks after we graduated from high school and we were just kids. You couldn't say we really knew what we were doing."

Gabe didn't say anything for a moment. They both stared at the pictures, and Gracie realized that the mention of her marriage somehow didn't seem out of place. It also didn't raise any guilt, even though she was sitting here with another man, having thoughts and feelings about him that were more than just platonic.

Then he said, "I don't know if you knew it or not but Adeline was worried that you were running away from your grief by going to Australia."

"I didn't run away from it. I ran away *with* it. I needed to go off by myself and live alone with all the feelings for a while, without well-meaning friends and relatives distracting me from it with activities or kindnesses. It's probably hard to understand, but I just needed to be someplace where memories didn't keep opening the wound and people didn't keep bandaging it up again. I needed to let it heal from the inside out."

He caught her eyes with his then. "And did you heal from the inside out?"

"For the most part."

That made him smile. "I'm glad to hear it," he said just before he leaned a little nearer. He tipped her chin with the slightest pressure of a curved index finger underneath, smiled a smile that seemed for her alone, and then he brought her mouth to his.

The first touch of his lips was warm and light—not tentative, just patient, as if letting her know he was willing to take it slowly. Then he slipped his hand to the back of her head and deepened the kiss.

He parted his lips over hers and she tasted the faint sweetness of the wine. His tongue persuaded her to relax and let him in—warm and wet, teasing and teaching all over again as if she were a novice.

It crossed Gracie's mind that it was very strange to be doing this with a man who wasn't Burt. But the thought didn't take any of the pleasure away from the act and so she let it drift out of her mind as smoothly as it had drifted in, freeing the way to just enjoy Gabe's kiss.

His arm came around her and pulled her close, and Gracie answered an urge of her own to press her hands against his chest. His pectorals were hard beneath the smooth knit of his shirt and she could feel his heartbeat against one palm—strong and steady and as alive as she felt.

He opened his mouth wider still and she welcomed his tongue with her own, matching him circle for circle, thrust for thrust.

Somewhere in the middle of the kiss her arms went around him and she held him as tightly as he held her, opening her mouth as wide as his was, and even chasing his tongue all the way back where she could boldly learn the velvety texture of the inside of his lips and the smoothness of his teeth.

She felt her nipples harden against his chest. The clothes that kept them from his skin suddenly seemed like armor and Gracie wanted them out of the way. Answering that, she slid her hands down his stomach, instinctively reaching for the tail of his shirt to pull up.

Then she stopped short, shocked at herself.

Struggling with her own aroused senses, Gracie broke away from the kiss. "Stop," she said in a breathy voice, as much to herself and her own careening desires as to Gabe.

That was all it took for him to let her go. His eyes closed for a moment and then opened as if he, too, had just remembered himself.

They were both silent long enough to gather their wits, then he reached a hand to the back of her head again, searching her face with those eyes of his from beneath drawn brows. "Are you okay?"

She nodded and even managed a weak smile.

"I better get out of here," he said. His fingers pulsed against her scalp. Then he let go, gathered the photograph albums and took her hand to bring her with him to the door.

"Are you sure you're all right?" he asked as if he wasn't completely convinced no matter what she said.

"I'm fine."

Once more he searched her eyes with his, then he kissed her again—quickly, fleetingly, as if he just couldn't resist.

"Good night," he said softly.

"Good night," she nearly whispered.

Then he left before she even remembered to thank him for the rest of what he'd done tonight.

And along with being frustrated, she was more than a little worried about the speed with which her feelings and desires for Gabe were growing.

Chapter Five

Within the span of twenty minutes the next morning, Gracie went from peacefully sipping hot lemon water as she sat on the porch step to the busy arrival of the appliance delivery truck and installation crew, the handyman Gabe had recommended, house painters and the lawn doctor.

And into this commotion shortly thereafter came Gabe.

She was in the living room, having just chosen the color she wanted the outside of the house painted, when he called through the screen. "Come on in," she called back.

But he wasn't alone. A very attractive older man followed him close behind.

Gracie took one look and knew who the other man was. "It's been a long time, but you have to be Eli Duran."

"Yes, on most days I do have to be," he answered with a smile. He had silver hair almost as thick as Gabe's, and they shared the same unusual blue eyes.

"We're about to take our walk but Pop wanted to thank you in person for the pictures." Gabe handed the albums to Gracie.

"That was quick," she said.

"I wasn't ready when he got there this morning so he went through them while I had my coffee," Gabe explained.

He watched her so intently that Gracie could almost feel his gaze, and it left her with a warm sensation. But she directed her question to Eli. "I hope you took all the pictures you wanted?"

"I did, thank you. I'm going to have them framed and put them out where I can see them. Maybe it will help missing Addie so much."

Gracie smiled at Eli referring to her aunt as Addie. No one else that Gracie had ever known had been allowed to use that diminutive.

Just then a burly man wheeled a dolly with the refrigerator strapped to it up to the front door. Both Gabe and Eli went to help. While Eli held the screen, Gabe offered to lift the entering end over the threshold while the delivery man pushed from the other side.

As Gabe worked, it was Gracie's turn to study him. He wore those old cutoffs and that tank top she'd noticed him in before, and seeing up close what the ragged clothes exposed was much more powerful than viewing it from a distance. Especially when his shoulders, biceps and the corded tendons of his forearms flexed to hoist the dolly's wheels.

He had to stretch his arms around the base of the refrigerator to get a grip, and that gave her a look at the hair under his arms—not a sight that ordinarily turned her on, and yet this morning it came very close.

Her lips suddenly felt hot and dry, and Gracie moistened them at the same time her gaze slid along the curve of his back to the arch of his tight rear end. When he was standing erect the cutoffs were short enough for the pockets to peek out the bottom through the frayed edges, but as he bent over those edges rode up high enough to hint at the bare buns underneath.

On the count of three he straddled the appliance, taking the weight on thighs that bulged and looked as if they could handle that and more. His calves were as hard as granite and low white socks stretched taut around his thickly boned ankles as he hoisted the refrigerator and dolly over the step and into the entry.

He'd been right about his shoes, though, she thought. They were godawful gray and worn. But even holey tennis shoes didn't neutralize what watching him aroused in her.

With the appliance inside now, Gabe guided it toward the kitchen. She knew she was gawking at him and that, short of letting her mouth gape open in hungry awe, it was probably obvious. And yet she couldn't pull her gaze off him as he slowly backed his way down the hall, careful not to nick the walls as he did.

Only when he was out of sight did she manage to look elsewhere. But elsewhere happened to be at Gabe's father, who had apparently closed the screen door and rejoined Gracie in the living room without her having noticed.

She hoped the older man had perceived her interest in the proceedings as new appliance appreciation. But he grinned and she knew he knew better. She smiled anyway, wishing she could think of something to say to segue out of this awkward moment.

He came to the rescue. "Gabe tells me you're trying to find someone who knew that Addie was selling him the comics."

"Yes, I am. In fact, I'm going to make some calls today. Do you have any suggestions about which of her friends I might start with?"

He did, and Gracie made a mental note of them.

"I don't blame you for wondering or wanting confirmation on Addie's intentions," he assured her then. "Even I could hardly believe it when Gabe told me about their arrangement. That woman thought it was some kind of sacrilege to part with most things, and certainly to sell anything. Especially something like the comics from way back in her past, something that had caught her fancy. Now if he'd have said she took those magazines out and got intrigued by them all over again the way I've seen her do a hundred times before, that I'd have believed without any trouble."

"Oh, she did that, too," Gabe said from the hallway, joining them and obviously having heard what his father was saying. "Adeline said she hadn't looked at the comics in years and when she took them out she started oohing and aahing over them."

"That was my Addie, all right."

"But in the end she agreed that I could sell them," Gabe said pointedly to Gracie.

Eli glanced at his watch. "We'd better get going." Then he took Gracie's hands in both of his. "Again, let me tell you how much those pictures of Addie and I together mean to me. I hate that she took herself off the way she did and ended our time together before it had to."

Gabe clapped a compelling hand to his father's shoulder. "We all hate it, Pop." Then to Gracie he said, "I have tickets to a concert at the Botanical Gardens tonight—bluegrass music, outdoors, and I'll pack the picnic dinner. Are you game?"

Gracie's first thought was that she should say no. Things between them were moving so far so fast it seemed logical that the pace should be slowed down.

And yet. Her time with him felt better than anything had in a long, long while. And he was only asking her to an outdoor concert, after all.

"Sounds great. I'd love to go."

"I'll be over at seven, then. Not a minute later."

"Good, because you're on probation," she teased him, going out onto the porch with the two men.

Murf was lying in the shade of one of the big trees and he didn't raise more than his eyebrows in acknowledgment of them.

"Come on, Murf, time to walk."

The dog groaned right on cue, and made them all laugh.

"Looks like you have more company," Eli said, nodding toward the car that had just pulled up between the handyman's truck and the lawn mower's trailer.

"That's my brother," she informed them as the short, slightly built man with Gracie's coloring and a more masculine version of her features headed toward them.

Dean and Eli had seen each other fairly recently, and only renewed their acquaintance, but Dean and Gabe had never met, so Gracie introduced them. When she did, Gabe held out his hand to her brother. She wondered if anyone else noticed Dean's split-second hesitation to take it, or the aloof way he studied Gabe.

But if Gabe saw or sensed anything amiss he didn't show it. Instead, when the amenities were over he said, "We were just on our way out." Then he turned back to Gracie with a smile. "I'll see you tonight."

"Pretty smooth character," Dean muttered as he and Gracie watched the threesome go.

Gracie didn't acknowledge the comment. Instead, she hugged him. "Oh, it's good to see you."

"You, too," he said, returning her hug.

"I didn't expect you so early in the morning. Since when are you up and about at this time of day?"

"I made a special exception just to see you." He nodded at the delivery truck. "Didn't you just go to buy appliances last night?"

"Yep," she confirmed. "But the owner of the store is a friend of Gabe's and I got preferential treatment—he pulled strings to get delivery first thing this morning." As they went into the house she offered her brother coffee.

"No, thanks. I just came to see you. And maybe the comic books."

"They're up in the attic."

"I know, you told me."

Gracie looked at him out of the corner of her eye. "Oh, I see. You're angling for a way to get up there."

"Could be."

"Come on, then."

"Oh, goody, goody." Dean rubbed his hands together like a glutton over a Boston cream pie.

They reached the uppermost floor, but while Gracie went into the attic, her brother stayed in the doorway, surveying the space from there.

"I can't tell you how many years it's been since Adeline let me up here," Dean said.

"However many years it's been since you started dealing antiques and bothering her about letting you sell
hers," Gracie told him. She went straight to the trunk.
"The comics are over here."

But Dean made it only partway into the attic before he
was drawn to the sideboard against one wall. He bent so
low over a scratch in the top that his nose nearly polished it out of the walnut surface.

"Dean?"

"Coming," he said without moving, instead opening
one of the cupboard doors. Then, as if he had to drag
himself away, he headed for the toy section where Gracie
was unpacking the trunk.

But he stalled at the horse tricycle. "Look at this," he
breathed rapturously. "You're going to renovate it, aren't
you?"

"It'll be my first project," she assured him.

"And you do such good work that no one will ever be
able to tell how dilapidated it was. Do you have any idea
what I could sell it for? Boggles the mind."

"Don't think about it, you'll just get depressed,"
Gracie advised with a laugh. "I thought you wanted to
see the comics?"

"We'll be such a good team, Gracie," he said, ignoring her question and instead squatting down to look at
the apron on the bottom of a chiffonier that stood to the
right of the tricycle. "I already have enough restorations
to keep you busy until next year. But imagine what we
could do with some of the things up here?"

"Dean—"

"I'm not even talking about the stuff in any of the
rooms below this. Just what's stashed away and hasn't
been used for decades."

She steadfastly refused to tell him what he already knew and instead said, "Come and look at the comics."

"Spoilsport." Dean finally joined her in front of the cedar chest just as she took the smaller wooden box out. "Oh, now there's a safe place to keep valuable original editions," he said facetiously. "I can understand addled Adeline doing it, but not you. Don't you know they should be in a safety deposit box, at least?"

"They've been safe here for over fifty years."

"Yes, but that was before some guy who apparently has access to your house knew they were here and wanted to get his grimy little hands on them."

"His hands are neither grimy nor little," she amended defensively.

Dean raised his eyebrows at that. "Excuse me—his big, clean, *manly* hands."

Her brother's ridiculous tone of voice made her laugh in spite of herself. "The last thing in the world Gabe would do is steal these comics."

"Is that right? Know him that well, do you?"

"I know him well enough to know that."

Dean took the magazines and carefully thumbed through them. When he'd finished he said, "I remembered something last night and made a few calls. The friend of the brother of a friend is an expert on these things."

"The friend of the brother of a friend? I won't even try to follow that."

"The important thing is that I'm going to contact him and talk to him so we have some basis from which to work—providing you find someone who confirms this *deal* between Adeline and her...your...friendly neighbor." He handed the comics back to her.

Gracie replaced them in the chest.

"So how come old Eli, of all people, doesn't know anything about the arrangement in question?"

Gracie explained Gabe's trying to spare his father worry.

"That's a little too convenient, isn't it? The single most likely person for our aunt to have told was the only one Duran wanted it kept from?"

"Gabe is very close to his father. He cares for him. I think it makes sense that he wouldn't want Eli worried about his financial problems."

"I just hope you're not being taken for a ride by this guy. You're too trusting, Gracie."

"As you and Willy can attest," she said facetiously.

"Amazing Gracie was a game we played on you as kids because you were so easy to fool. We could tell you anything and you'd believe it. But this is no game."

"I was seven years old. You and Willy were twelve—of course, I believed what you told me. That doesn't have a bearing on anything now."

"Doesn't it? You've always trusted everyone. Too much. I just don't want you to get hurt."

"Are we talking about the comics or something else?"

"I'm talking about the comics *and* something else. If you sell this guy the comics and then find out he was lying you'll hate yourself—I know you. And as for the something else, well, you have to admit that after fifteen years of marriage to your high-school sweetheart you aren't very single-wise."

"Single-wise?" she repeated. "Which means what? That I should be cynical and suspicious? Come on, Dean."

"I'm speaking from experience."

"I know you are," she answered sympathetically. It was true that Dean had not been lucky in love.

"There are a lot of people out there with a lot of different motives and agendas, Gracie. If this guy's business is in trouble and he's convinced the comics are his ticket to salvaging it, that's a pretty powerful reason to do and say anything to get his hands on them. Even if it means playing with your emotions."

She couldn't deny that Gabe had a strong need for the comics, because it was true; but as for the idea that the personal side of their relationship was a ploy to accomplish his necessary ends, Gracie just couldn't accept that. "I'm being careful," she told her brother.

His expression said he didn't buy that for a minute. "I hope so, but don't get mad at me for looking out for you. And part of doing that is with this comic-book business. I'm going to check with the expert I've located to find out all I can about this sort of thing, and I'm keeping my eye on what evolves with it."

"In other words, the comics are going to be your divining rod—if everything looks like it's on the up-and-up with them it'll help you believe he's just charmed by me?" she teased.

"Anybody could be charmed by you," he teased. Then his tone turned more serious again. "But yeah, I'll feel a lot better if it turns out this is on the up-and-up. Give me someone who heard from Adeline's own lips that she was selling the comics to this guy and I'll feel almost good about him."

"Almost good?"

Dean shrugged. "I'll still be a little worried that it's too soon for you to be involved with anyone."

Gracie rolled her eyes. "I think you're just a compulsive worrier."

Towel drying his hair after his post-walk shower, Gabe stepped from the bathroom into his bedroom to check the time. Nine-thirty. He opened The Collector's Exchange at ten, and in order to make it today he needed to speed up.

He dropped his hair-drying towel to the floor and went to the bureau for his brush, a second towel still slung around his hips. He should have just sent his father across the street alone after their walk instead of going with Eli before, he knew. But if he'd done that he would have missed seeing Gracie.

"I've got it bad for her," he told his reflection in the mirror. So bad that he wasn't even closing his bedroom drapes anymore at night. Instead, he lay on his side in bed and watched her lights turn off downstairs one by one, picturing her in his mind as she made her way upstairs to turn on the lamp in her bedroom.

It was a masochistic practice. By the time that bedroom lamp was turned on so was he.

Of course, kissing her when they said good-night didn't help matters. God, but he loved the way she kissed. Her lips were so damned soft. And sweet. She fit so well between his arms, against his chest, her small breasts molding to him. . . .

His right arm started to fall asleep and he realized suddenly that while his thoughts had wandered he'd been holding his brush poised above his head, not moving a muscle. He finished combing his hair.

He also liked waking up in the morning now with the drapes open. That way all he had to do was roll over to catch his first glimpse of Gracie's house, and sometimes of Gracie.

Like today. She'd been sitting on her porch steps, her arms hugging her knees, sipping something steamy from a mug. What a sight to wake up to. The sun had made her shiny hair blush, looking as silky as it felt on those few occasions when he'd managed to get his hands in it.

She'd been wearing jeans and a shapeless T-shirt that hid her curves, but she was barefoot and for some reason his gaze had caught on her long, thin feet curved over the top of the step below where she sat. He'd watched her curl her toes up and down every so often, seemingly unaware of what she was doing. Absolutely unaware of what such a simple sight as her naked, pink-hued feet did to tighten his insides.

Shaking himself out of his reverie a second time, he pushed away from the bureau and stepped into the closet where he let the towel around his waist fall and pulled on a pair of jeans. Then, slipping into his shirt, he went back into the room.

But halfway through fastening the buttons he caught sight of Gracie as she came out of the house with the handyman. The two of them stopped just outside her front door, obviously to discuss the screen. The problem was self-evident, and when the handyman took over she turned her back directly into Gabe's line of vision.

The first thing his gaze did was drop to her rear end. The legs of her jeans were loose but the seat cupped her small derriere almost as tightly as his palms ached to. He imagined himself pulling her hips up close to his. Then she slid both of her hands into the back pockets of her jeans and sweat broke out along his upper lip.

He took a deep breath, closed his eyes and forced his head to turn until his chin was nearly on his shoulder. Then he blew out the breath and opened his eyes. The first thing they settled on was the bedside clock. It was five minutes after ten.

He was late. And uncomfortably turned on—even if all her lights were off.

Oh, what he wouldn't give to have her right there in that room with him at that moment. With the drapes closed. And his hands in her pockets.

It had certainly been a lot easier to go to work in the mornings when a glance across the street just meant seeing wiry, white-haired Adeline. Maybe leaving the drapes open wasn't such a good idea, after all.

He jammed his wallet into his back pocket and grabbed his keys, glad that Murf was already in the backyard so he didn't have to lose any more time coaxing the dog outside. One glance at the back door and the front told him they were both locked, so he barged through the one to the garage.

"Sorry, car, can't let you idle for even a minute today," he said as he started the engine and slammed it into reverse, pushing the button to open the garage door as he did. As it automatically began to rise he let the car start to roll backward and then glanced out his rearview mirror.

There was a car in his driveway.

He slammed on the brake to keep from hitting it and let rip a pretty choice expletive before he got out of the car at the same time as a gorgeous woman he'd never seen before.

"Gabe Duran?" she asked with a blinding flash of white teeth and a toss of her blond hair.

"That's me."

She reached into the purse hanging from a shoulder strap to bounce against the hint of a hip hugged by black bicycle shorts. Taking an envelope out, she handed it to him. "Have a nice day," she said, turning back to her car.

"What is this?"

She shrugged artfully. "Notice that you're being sued," she said as happily as if she were telling him he'd won a grand prize.

Then she got into her car and left.

The expletive this time made the other one pale by comparison.

The Collector's Exchange would have to wait. He opened the envelope and took out the papers inside. He'd read enough legal documents during his corporate days to be able to glance over this one and realize that Simonesque was handling the suit for the group of collectors the lawyer belonged to. That was as far as Gabe bothered to go before hightailing it back into the house, searching for the attorney's phone number and dialing it.

While he waited for the secretary to see if Simonesque was in, he calmed down. Some.

"Mr. Duran," the lawyer said when he came on the line. "What can I do for you?"

Simonesque's voice made it clear he was enjoying this. It allowed Gabe to sound calmer and cooler than he felt, rather than let the lawyer get the best of him. "I just had a visit from a beautiful blonde I think you're familiar with. She hand-delivered notice of a lawsuit. Want to tell me what this is for?"

"Inspiration," Simonesque said coyly.

"Inspiration," Gabe repeated, almost losing his cool. "Inspiration for what?"

"To come up with those comic books."

There was no enthusiasm in Gracie's dressing for the concert that evening. She halfheartedly chose a long, oversize pink mock turtleneck and a pair of black capri-length leggings.

All the while she dressed and combed her hair, Dean's words came back to haunt her. He was right; she wasn't single-wise.

Wouldn't a single-wise person have asked Gabe up front about other women he might be involved with?

Gracie thought they would have, and she wished she had.

Or maybe a single-wise person would just assume an attractive, unmarried man saw other women.

Maybe. Maybe experienced single women became accustomed to other women being in the lives of single men.

But Gracie didn't think that was something she'd ever be able to handle without feeling rotten. As rotten as she felt now.

Tall, leggy, beautiful blondes, she had discovered this morning, were tough on mortal women's egos. Especially when they drove their sporty little cars right up onto a man's driveway as if they did it every day, and were met by that man with a smile on his face.

What had happened after that, Gracie didn't know. She'd gone inside rather than witness any more.

She felt naive and inexperienced—just what Dean was worried she was. Of course, Gabe had other women in his life. Of course, they were beautiful. "What did you think—that he was cloistered in the house across the street the way Adeline is in Tibet?" she asked herself as she slipped her feet into black flats.

But recognizing that Gabe owed her no allegiance or loyalty didn't make her feel any better. And when she admitted to herself that this bad feeling was jealousy, it didn't help matters.

At two minutes before seven her doorbell rang.

As she went to answer it, Gracie reminded herself that she and Gabe were not a couple, that two kisses probably didn't mean anything more to the average single person than sitting next to a stranger in a movie theater did, and that she and Gabe certainly did not have an agreement that their relationship included exclusivity. She also gave herself a stern talking to about having been a widow for only six months and not being ready for any kind of actual involvement with any man anyway, whether he had other women in his life, or not.

"Hi," she said when she opened the door to Gabe, hating that the greeting came out so dispiritedly.

He made a show of looking at his watch. "I want you to notice that I'm right on time."

"Duly noted." And much too formally spoken.

Gabe frowned. "Is everything all right?"

She pasted a smile on her face. "Sure. Do you want to come in or shall we go?"

"I'm ready if you are." He opened the screen, being more careful with it than he needed to be.

"The handyman you recommended fixed it this morning," she told him.

"That's right. I forgot that I saw him over here."

As they walked out to his car, Gabe took her hand, pulling her closer than she'd originally been. "You look great tonight," he said, his mouth close enough to her ear for her to feel the warmth of his breath against it.

"Thanks," she answered, hating the sudden memory of Dean's suggestion that Gabe could be playing with her emotions in order to get the comics. She'd been so sure that wasn't the case when her brother had said it, but seeing that blonde in Gabe's driveway an hour later had shot a great big hole in her certainty.

Gabe opened the car door for her and then went around the front to his own. Gracie was staring straight ahead, trying not to look at him because one sight always weakened her knees. But even in the instant that he passed through her line of vision she registered the fact that he wore white tennis shorts and a yellow polo shirt that accentuated his dark coloring.

"I spent the afternoon making calls to Adeline's friends to see if anyone knew about your deal with her," she said as Gabe wheeled the car away from the curb. It was all she could think to talk about that might not give away her feelings.

"I certainly hope somebody knew about it."

"No, no one did." She'd heard a lot of stories about things her aunt had given friends—tokens of appreciation, mementos, things of Adeline's that they'd admired or needed that they found on their doorstep the morning after having let her know. But not a soul had any idea of the arrangement over the comic books. And to a person they had all found it hard to believe Adeline would sell anything. But Gracie didn't add that. Instead, she said, "I'm sorry."

"So am I."

There was something odd in his voice that she couldn't quite name. She glanced over at him, seeing the muscle in his jaw tighten like a pulse beat.

Then he said, "I have another problem over those comics. The group of collectors who were going to buy them is suing me because I haven't delivered."

"Can they do that?"

He inclined his head and breathed a mirthless laugh. "Oh, yes, they can definitely do that. You see, they owned several comic books that weren't as important as Baby Jack Flash but carried a reasonably high value. I persuaded them to sell the lesser issues in order to raise some of the money for Adeline's . . . sorry, yours. I even handled the sale. Now they're claiming that I misled them into believing that the Baby Jack Flash issues were available when they weren't in order to get them to sell what they otherwise wouldn't have.''

"Have you called a lawyer?"

He nodded. "The bottom line is that either I need to get them the comics or at least prove I acted in good faith because selling them was Adeline's intention."

"When did you find out about this?"

"This morning. In fact, the attorney who's handling the suit—his name is Simonesque and he's a member of the group and a real pain in the butt—thought it was funny to have me served with the papers by some young blond bombshell."

"The girl in the red car this morning?" The words flooded out of Gracie's mouth before she could stop them.

Gabe took his eyes off the highway for a moment to glance at her. "That's the one."

Gracie's head went light with relief. She felt a little giddy she was so glad to find out that the blonde hadn't been another woman in Gabe's life. Then, a moment later, she felt guilty for being so elated over something that was the harbinger of more bad luck for him. And she still wasn't in a position to offer any help.

"I have a few more numbers in Adeline's address book to call and Willy is checking with the relatives. All hope of someone turning up who knows about this isn't lost."

He didn't look consoled. "Speaking of lawyers—how about Adeline's? Are you checking with him?"

"I hadn't thought about it," she admitted. "And I didn't come across his name in the address book, so no, he wasn't one of the people I was calling. Do you think he might know something?"

"I think it's worth a try. At this point, anything is."

Gabe pulled to a stop behind another car going into the parking lot at the Botanical Gardens and reached over to take Gracie's hand. "This lawsuit has been on my mind all day long and I'm sick of thinking about it. Let's put it on hold so we can both have a good time tonight."

Gracie was more than willing to agree to that.

They shared fried chicken, potato chips, grapes and wine for dinner as they waited for the concert to begin. While they ate it occurred to Gracie that the blonde being a summons server had been a reprieve and that it was about time to practice a little single-wisdom.

"You know," she said without looking at Gabe where he sat across from her on a blanket spread on the lawn, "I thought maybe the girl in your driveway this morning was a friend."

He didn't say anything for a minute and Gracie could feel him watching her. When she glanced at him she found him smiling. "You thought she was a *girlfriend*," he accused.

"No, I knew she was a girl. I could see that," she joked. "But I assumed she was a friend."

"And were you just a little jealous? Is that why you were so stiff when I picked you up tonight?"

"No." She was quick to deny that she was just a little jealous. In truth she'd been a lot jealous. "I was not stiff when you picked me up."

"Cold and brittle, then," he claimed, barely keeping the amusement out of his voice while the glitter in his blue eyes gave him away.

"I beg your pardon. I am never cold or brittle." She pretended affront, smiling in spite of herself. "Thinking that she was a friend did make me wonder, though."

"About?"

"Other women in your life."

"Past or present?" he said easily, leaning back on his elbows and looking at her from under his eyebrows as if he didn't have a thing to hide and was just waiting for the category to be opened.

"Both," she challenged.

"There have definitely been women in my life in the past," he teased.

"Very funny. And if there have been these women in your past why haven't you ever married any of them?"

"My father does enough of that for both of us," he answered glibly. "But the past should not be what you're asking about, because that's over," he counseled.

"What should I be asking about, then?"

"The present. You're supposed to ask me if I'm involved—seriously or otherwise—with anyone now."

"Okay, I'm asking."

"And I'm answering. Yes."

A big lump suddenly formed in Gracie's throat. "Oh," she said, wishing she hadn't when it came out sounding hurt.

"She's a new neighbor of mine. Just moved in on Monday night. Sort of on the short side, great hair the color of peaches and cream, beautiful eyes, and lips that are the sweetest I've ever tasted."

"And you're cheating on her with me?" she bantered to hide the mixture of embarrassment and pleasure over his description of her.

"How about your romantic history?"

"I was married for fifteen years," she informed him as if it was news.

"No kidding?" he deadpanned.

"But other than that—I'd never dated anyone before Burt, or since."

"Wow. Not many people can say that."

And maybe she shouldn't have, either, Gracie thought.

Gabe sat up suddenly and clasped his hand around the back of her neck, pulling her nose to his. "Well, I am not now, nor have I been in the past year, involved with a woman other than you. I'm afraid I can't narrow the field down to your one past serious relationship, but I can assure you that there's nothing recent or ongoing. Okay?"

She couldn't help smiling. "Okay," she said.

For a moment they stared into each other's eyes, and then the bluegrass band came out onto the platform at the base of the knoll on which they were sitting. The crowd rearranged itself on its various blankets to face the music. Gabe took Gracie by the shoulders and turned her so that her back was to him, pulling her to lean against him just as the first chords of a banjo duet echoed against the glass walls of the indoor gardens behind them.

She had been pretty silly, Gracie decided, to feel and think the things she had about the blonde. But those thoughts and feelings were very telling, she realized now. And what they told her was that a mere six months into widowhood or not, she was definitely involved with this man.

It was after midnight by the time Gracie and Gabe got home. Too late to expect to be asked in, Gabe thought, too late to accept even if Gracie extended the invitation. But that didn't stop him from wishing the evening didn't have to end as he got out of the car in his garage and went around to Gracie's door.

He kept his arm at her waist as he walked her across the street, holding her close to his side. She had a power over him, he thought. The power to put even the biggest of his problems on the back burner of his mind. The power to make him feel good at the worst of times. No one had ever done that before.

They climbed her porch steps. He took her keys from her hand and unlocked the front door. But he didn't let go of her so she could go in. Not yet. He wasn't ready to lose her company no matter how late it was.

Bracing the screen against his backside he turned her to face him, leaving both of his arms draped over her shoulders, and dropping his forehead to hers. "How about if I get my father to work the shop tomorrow and I come help you move your things in from the garage?"

"You don't have to do that. I wasn't hinting for help when I said that was what I was doing tomorrow. I was going to call my brother."

"I didn't think you were hinting for help. I'm offering because I want to see you." He thought that her small, tired smile was the nicest thing he'd seen all day.

"Isn't Saturday a bad time for you to take off?"

"I have a man who comes in to work it with me. Between him and my father they can handle it."

"Okay."

"Okay." He curled his arms around her and brought her in close against him, setting his chin on the top of her head just so he could breathe in the scent of her hair one more time tonight. "When do you want me?" he asked, smiling a little at the double entendre he'd unintentionally made that sound like.

"There's no rush."

That's what you think. You'd know better if you had any idea what's happening inside me right now. "Around ten, then?"

"Sounds good."

So did her voice, a little huskier than it had been a moment before. Maybe she did know what was happening inside him.

He leaned back enough to look into her face. God, how he wanted her.

She tipped her chin up toward him and he couldn't resist those pale lips any longer. He took them between his own, and that first touch of her warm, satin mouth was like answering a craving that gnawed at him. He held the back of her head so he could press harder, delve deeper, feeling the smooth silk of her hair against his palm.

Her tongue met his and danced a circle with him that only made him want more of her, and he knew it was a good thing they were standing in the glow of her porch light. Anywhere more comfortable, more private, and he might forget things he needed to remember. Things like how new he was to her.

Still, though, he had to hold her a little tighter, he had to have her a little closer, he had to feel her breasts against his chest, her hips against his.

It was torture not being able to take this further. To let it find the natural end it deserved. But it was glorious torture and he almost let it go on beyond the point of no return.

On the verge of that he stopped.

He lifted his head away from her, looking down at her face, seeing just how hard he'd kissed her in the slight puffiness to her lips. And for one split second he very nearly answered the urge to pick her up and carry her inside.

"Good night, Gracie," he managed to grind out, hearing the agony in his own voice as clearly as he felt it in his body.

She didn't answer him. He didn't think she could because she looked as overwhelmed with wanting as he was. Instead she nodded, and those great wide eyes of hers accused him of inflicting the same frustrations on her that he was suffering himself.

"Good night," he whispered again, forcing his arms to let her go. "I'll be back in the morning."

He stepped out of the door, holding the screen while she went inside, and then firmly replacing it in the frame even though now that it was fixed it was unnecessary.

Then he waved a single, feeble wave, turned and lit out for home and the coldest damn shower he could take, thinking that at least he'd be back with her in a few hours' time. And even if it was only to move furniture, it was worth it.

He reached his own house, going in through the garage. But somehow closing the garage door reminded him of that morning and finding the summons server in his driveway. The memory brought the Baby Jack Flash comic books back into his thoughts. And realizing all over again how much he had on the line took the place of the shower.

Chapter Six

Gracie passed up her usual cup of hot lemon water the next morning in favor of a mug of high-octane coffee. She needed the caffeine. And after her bath, instead of only her usual application of blush, she was also going to need a heavy helping of concealer to hide the dark circles under her eyes.

Sexual frustration, she'd learned the night before, did, indeed, cause physical discomfort, tension, anxiousness and lack of sleep.

She'd discovered about a month ago that a widow's lack of sex drive lasted only so long. And then the absence of a love life that had been good for fifteen years really hit home. Top that off with meeting an attractive man who kissed better than anyone she'd ever known and Gracie was having a tough time keeping herself under control.

As she poured her second cup of coffee another thought occurred to her—was it possible her attraction to Gabe was simply lust?

Lust was definitely alive and well inside her. But it wasn't as if Gabe was nothing more than a sex object to her. She enjoyed his company too much for that to be true. He made her laugh. She felt comfortable with him, free to be herself, accepted, liked. They had a good time together.

The fact that he made her hormones perk was just frosting on the cake.

She caught sight of herself in the side of the toaster, and red-rimmed eyes stared back at her. Was this the look of sex starvation? Had she partaken of that particular frosting last night would she have gotten up feeling and looking much better this morning?

But what did that mean? That she should hop into bed with Gabe? Had their relationship really gone that far? Could this even be called a relationship after less than a week?

She was involved with him—she'd realized that last night. Involvement should certainly qualify as a relationship. And the relationship had gone far enough for her to want him to make love to her; she couldn't deny that, especially not with the past sleepless night to call her a liar if she did.

But was she ready to go to bed with him? With a man who wasn't Burt?

She suddenly couldn't swallow the drink of coffee she'd just taken. Shivers ran up her arms. There was ringing in her ears. She felt light-headed and her heart was pounding so fast and hard she could feel it.

Panic. Pure, unadulterated panic.

What could she be thinking of? Kissing was one thing. But making love?

She finally managed to swallow her coffee.

"Oh-my-gosh."

Making love was a whole other consideration. Clothes were taken off. She didn't have a nineteen-year-old's body anymore. A certain amount of expertise would be expected from her—she wasn't a virgin, after all—but she'd never made love with anyone but Burt. Her experience was limited. And in this new age that wasn't an asset.

She couldn't do it. That was all there was to it. The body was willing but the mind knew better.

Gabe might be nice and great looking. He might make her laugh and show her a good time. He might even kiss well enough to make her forget things she should remember. But he was still a virtual stranger. And she'd been a widow for only six months. Six short months.

Gracie rinsed her cup and put it in the dishwasher. Then she headed down the hallway, intent on going upstairs for her bath. As she reached the entrance she could see Gabe just leaving his house with his father and Murf for their walk.

And suddenly it occurred to her that he hadn't asked to make love to her. He hadn't done anything but kiss her. And last night, just when she had been lost in that kiss—*he* had stopped it.

Who said he even wanted to make love to her?

That kiss had. And the way he'd held her.

At least she thought so.

But maybe she was wrong. Maybe these things were like learning a foreign language—without using the skill for a while a person could misinterpret.

She watched Gabe walk beyond where she could see him without once even glancing in the direction of her house. It definitely seemed possible that she was jumping the gun. That she was the only one of them thinking of making love just because they'd shared a few kisses. Glorious kisses. But just kisses.

"You've gone nuts, Gracie. Completely around the bend," she told herself as she climbed the stairs. Because as much as the thought of making love with Gabe scared her, the thought that he didn't want to disappointed her.

She took clean towels from the armoire in the big bathroom, considering the emotional roller-coaster ride of the past few minutes. Bad sign, she thought.

One of the phenomena of grief—the erratic ups and downs—hadn't happened to her in a long time. Maybe the recurrence was a warning that she might not be as far away from the grieving process as it seemed.

Then again, weren't erratic ups and downs also a phenomenon of love?

Love?

Oh, no, it was definitely too soon for that.

A full year was the amount of time the grief books and counselors and people who had gone through the loss of a close loved one claimed it took to really be back to normal. The rule of thumb was that no big decisions should be made during that year.

She'd already blown that by selling the house in Connecticut, going to Australia and now moving back to Denver. Not that any of those decisions had so far proven bad. But none involved her heart, either. And Gabe did.

Gracie sank into a steamy bubble bath, realizing that whether it was ill-advised or not, her heart already had a soft spot in it for Gabe. She cared about him. And all that was left now was for her to hope the early arrival of that didn't prove bad, either.

But the suddenness of feelings for him, unlike her other decisions, worried her.

"Are you sure about this, Gracie?" Gabe asked when he'd raised her garage door and stood looking at what was inside.

"Nothing else has worked. I can't seem to make up my mind what of Adeline's furniture I want to use and what of my own. So I thought I'd move most of my stuff in, too, see how I can mix and mingle, and try making up my mind when I'm looking at what works and what doesn't."

"Maybe you should consider reinforcing the floor-boards first."

"Did you come over here to help or to be a wise guy?"

"To be a wise guy," he answered like one. Then, still staring at the furniture and boxes packing the double wide garage, he shook his head. "Adeline was right—you are as much of a pack rat as she is. And some of these things look heavy. I'm not sure you're strong enough to move them."

She made a muscle. "Sure I am. Besides, I have two dollies. We could move mountains with those."

His expression said we'll see. "Okay, then, where do we start?"

She picked up a box marked Linens and headed for the house. "With what's in front," she told him, cracking wise herself. "We can put all the boxes in the kitchen. I've already decided to keep my aunt's table and chairs. My own set is just a plain, serviceable Formica table and some chairs that have seen better days. They don't compare to Adeline's oak pedestal and ladder-backs."

Gabe took a box under each arm and followed her inside. "And what will you do with yours? Get rid of it?" he asked hopefully.

"I'll use it for a worktable. The garage is big enough for my car, my tools and a work space, too."

"Well, at least that's one thing we won't have to move," he said wryly, setting his boxes beside hers on the countertop before going back outside for more.

This time it was Gracie who followed Gabe, and as she did her gaze attached itself to him. He had on a pair of well-worn jean shorts and a plain blue T-shirt, but he did them both justice. His tight rear end fit into the shorts as if they'd been tailored for him, and the knit of the T-shirt molded to his broad shoulders.

When he picked up two more boxes, she couldn't resist taking a peek at the taut bulges of his biceps and forearms, and at the span of his chest in between what he carried.

"Get your buns in gear, Canon," he ordered when her distraction made her lag behind.

On this trip she gave a close study to his bare legs. They were hairy and muscular above his tennis socks and shoes. "Boy, do you have knobby knees," she told him in the kitchen, teasing him to get back for his buns-in-gear remark.

He tipped his head to one side and studied her knees, bared by black short shorts. "Well, yours aren't too bad. But don't get me started on your feet," he said after a moment.

She glanced down at her black leather tennis shoes. "I know. Size nine and a half. It means I have a good understanding."

"Of what?" He laughed, holding the back door open for her to precede him outside again.

"Men with knobby knees."

He tossed a mock dirty look at her and she caught his eyes dropping for just a split second to her breasts where they were crushed nearly flat by the spandex leotard she wore. Then he grabbed her in a playful headlock and said, "Yeah? Well, understand this. I don't work for anybody who doesn't like my knees, so take it back."

"They're the most beautiful knees I've ever seen," she professed elaborately.

"That's better," he said, releasing the headlock but keeping his arm across her shoulders as they faced the garage again.

With all the boxes off her old kitchen table, they moved it out onto the driveway and faced the next layer—a king-size mattress set and headboard.

"I don't suppose you know anybody who wants a bed, do you?"

He looked shocked. "As in parting with something? You?" he teased.

But this wasn't a joke to Gracie and she couldn't hide the stab that went through her to look at the bed she and Burt had shared. "It bothers me too much to keep it. I haven't slept in it even once since the accident."

His expression immediately turned knowing and sympathetic, and his tone went with it, keeping just enough of a light edge to smooth this difficult moment. "As a matter of fact, I do know someone who would love to have it. What do you say we move it over to my garage and I'll take care of it from there?"

It was silly, but she felt her eyes fill with tears. Not over the bed, but over his kindness and understanding of her feelings. She managed a smile when she'd swallowed the lump in her throat. "You're all right for a guy with knobby knees, anyone ever tell you that?'' she said in a soft, heartfelt tone.

"Yeah, well, you're all right for a lady with big feet,'' he answered her the same way, stretching his arm across her shoulders again to pull her close into his side so he could kiss her forehead. Then he gave her a tight squeeze and let go. "Come on, let's get it out of here.''

When they had relocated the bed they could get several feet into the garage. Next in line were two small armless cream-colored chairs with pleated ruffles around the bottoms and tufted backs.

"These go upstairs in the bathroom,'' she said.

"Chairs in the bathroom? What are you going to do—hang them from the ceiling?''

"There's plenty of room.'' Gracie picked up one of them.

"In the bathroom?'' he repeated as if he thought she'd meant to say something else.

"You have seen the bathroom, haven't you?''

"The one downstairs. But a bathroom is a bathroom.''

Gracie smiled. "Boy, do you have a surprise coming.''

Once they had the chairs upstairs she went into the greenhouselike bathroom. Gabe only made it as far as the door. He stopped cold, letting his gaze make a slow circle around the room. "Incredible. I can't believe I never knew this was up here.''

"Don't feel bad. I doubt if too many of Adeline's friends, especially those who were male, would have had occasion to use either of the bedrooms or the bathroom on this floor.'' Gracie took the second chair from him. She'd put the first one beside the armoire; this one she set next to the pedestal sink.

"This is like something out of *House Beautiful*.''

"What? This old thing? I thought you were only impressed with what's new and modern," she goaded.

He finally stepped into the room, checking out the claw-footed bathtub, poking his head into the alcove where the toilet was, and ending up at the windows that faced the backyard and the enormous trees that grew higher than the glass-and-beamed ceiling. "Okay, I'm impressed."

He went back to the tub and traced the edge with his thumb, giving Gracie a sidelong, lascivious look. "This is the stuff fantasies are made of." Then he leaned against one of the oak columns, crossed his right foot over the other and nodded to the tub. "Want to fulfill a few of mine?"

"Not a chance." She pretended to crack an imaginary whip. "Back to the garage, slave."

His smile was slow and sexy. "You'll never know what you're missing."

Downstairs again, Gracie explained that she wanted to move her aunt's small television up to the master bedroom so she could use her larger, newer model in the living room. Gabe did that himself while she moved some of the furniture to make space for her own living-room things, which were next in line in the garage.

But before they tackled that they agreed to take a breather from the afternoon heat and so many trips back and forth. Gracie gave Gabe a beer, poured a glass of iced tea for herself, and they took them to sit in the shade of one of the trees in the front yard.

While they rested and enjoyed a midafternoon breeze, Gabe pointed out each house in the neighborhood and gave her a thumbnail sketch of the owners, most of the time making her laugh at his descriptions.

"Oh, I almost forgot," she said when he'd covered the whole block. "I found the home phone number for Adeline's lawyer and called this morning."

"And?"

"He's out of town until sometime next week."

"Thank God. I thought you were going to say he was a dead end, too."

"I'll call his office first thing Monday and leave the same message I left at his house just in case he doesn't get it there—that I need to talk to him as soon as possible when he gets back."

Gabe smoothed her hair behind her ear. "I appreciate it. Those papers on the lawsuit keep staring at me with evil eyes," he said. Then he got to his feet and helped Gracie up. "I better get back to work to earn the trouble I'm putting you to."

In the garage once again, Gabe repeated his skepticism about adding Gracie's sofa, chair, end tables, coffee table, lamps and bookcases to Adeline's already full parlor. But Gracie insisted.

First went the sofa, a much less formal piece than the velvet, tufted one already there. Once they managed to get it into the living room, Gabe sat on the overstuffed cream-colored couch and put his vote in for keeping it instead of Adeline's. And when they brought the matching chair in he advised using that instead of the big maroon high-backed one.

"I may use my sofa, but I love that old chair of Adeline's. It's as cozy as an oyster in a shell for curling up with a book in front of the fire on a snowy day. Let's put my chair in the bedroom upstairs."

As they did that, Gabe said, "Once you make up your mind about the keepers, what are you going to do with the rest?"

"I wish I knew. I think I'll try to consolidate what's already in the attic to make space up there. And maybe some things can go into the rafters of the garage."

"You could rent a storage space and put the extra furniture there. But I have to tell you I think it's crazy not to keep what you want and unload the rest regardless of what Adeline said. Maybe she was getting a little senile when she devised that will, and no one realized it. I just don't see the point."

They left the chair in a corner of the master bedroom and went back out to the garage.

"My aunt was not senile. She just loved her things and didn't want to see them unloaded, as you put it—trashed, as Willy puts it—or sold off to just anybody by my brother, who has been itching to do that ever since he went into the antique business. And I understand her feelings."

"But Gracie," he reasoned with exaggerated patience. "Even if you store it all until you die, what's going to happen to it then? It'll be unloaded, trashed or sold, anyway. Unless you plan to leave a trust fund to pay for its keep until the end of time."

Gracie took an end table, and Gabe took the other one and a section of bookcase.

"I'll do the same thing Adeline would have done with it had she not decided so suddenly to cut her earthly ties. Whenever I come across someone who would appreciate and care for something the way she—or I—would, I'll give it to them." Then she added a little more softly, "And who knows, maybe someday I'll have kids and as they're starting out on their own I'll be able to pass things on to them that they can pass down to their kids."

Neither of them said anything else as they went back to the garage, but when they brought in what was left of the living-room things Gabe went on, "Adeline always wondered how come you didn't have a baby."

Gracie could tell that it wasn't her aunt who had wondered about her childlessness as much as Gabe did now. But she didn't mind. "Getting pregnant just never happened," she said, making it sound so much more simple than the infertility had been.

"Did you want one?"

"Sure."

"Did your husband?"

"Yes." With a mazelike maneuver she went to the end tables to set the lamps down. "What about you? Don't you ever want to have kids?"

"If I can have more than one I'd like to, yes," he answered, high-stepping over a section of bookcase to the only free spot in the room where he could set the coffee table.

"What would be wrong with having just one?"

He shrugged those broad shoulders of his. "I hated being an only child. Every time my father got married again I'd hope like crazy for a brother."

"A sister wouldn't have counted?"

"Depended on the season. Baseball and football season I'd pray for a brother. Over the holidays I would have even been happy with a sister."

Gracie laughed. "But only as a last resort."

"Hey, I was a kid," was his only defense. "It took some time before I learned to appreciate girls." He looked her up and down. "But, boy, do I appreciate them now. Especially when I have them where I want them."

He had her boxed in, Gracie realized when she looked around. He'd put the coffee table in the last clear path. "You'd have been an evil big brother."

"Probably."

"Are you going to let me out of here?"

"For a price—one big, juicy wet kiss."

"Yuk."

"Pay or stay."

She made her way to face him on the other side of the coffee table and puckered up.

"Prune face," he taunted before taking her by the shoulders and planting a big, juicy kiss on her lips.

Gracie made an even worse face. "Now will you let me out of here so we can finish this before midnight tonight?"

He pretended to think about it. Then he reached to grasp her sides in both hands and lifted her over the low table.

But once he had her on his side he didn't set her on her feet. He only lowered her far enough for them to be on eye level. Her hands were on his shoulders and she could feel the solid bulges of his muscles beneath them. There was no sign of any strain in his bearing her weight. Instead, his incredible blue eyes penetrated hers just before he kissed her again, this time softly, setting off little sparks in the pit of her stomach in the instant that the warmth of his lips met hers.

He brought her body against his and let her slide like hot lava down a mountain until her feet touched the floor again.

"Maybe we should take another break," he said, his tone suggesting more than his words, his arms wrapped around her.

"Maybe we shouldn't," she answered, but there wasn't much force behind it.

He smiled—a slow, lopsided thing that lingered there while his eyes dropped to her mouth as if he was considering his options.

Then his smile turned into a grin. He let go of her and turned to step over the arm of one of the sofas to get out. "Quit distracting me from my work," he accused, reaching back to take her hand so she could climb out, too.

She did, but with a ten-second delay on her reaction time.

"Now," he said. "Make up your mind about these couches so we can take one of them out to the garage, or you'll never be able to move anything around in here to see what you're keeping and what you're not."

After a moment spent more in restraining her thoughts than in decision making, Gracie pointed to Adeline's. "As much as I love it, it just isn't as comfortable as mine."

Without thinking of anything more than getting to the opposite end, she climbed over the arm and crawled along the tufted cushions.

"Tempting. Very tempting."

She wasn't sure she'd heard him and glanced over her shoulder to find him staring at her derriere. "Dirty old man," she called him. But he only smiled beatifically.

Once they had the sofa outside Gracie meticulously covered it with a tarp before they set it out of the way in the garage.

Next came a stacked toolbox, a workbench, two table saws and several drills and hand tools. "Somehow you don't look like a lady who'd own a jigsaw," he said.

"How do lady jigsaw owners look?" she countered.

He eyed her up and down. "Not like that," he answered appreciatively.

"You know what I think? I think you're stalling," she accused, glancing at the only piece of furniture left to be moved into the house—an armoire that was a full foot taller than he was.

His grin gave him away. "You have to admit that there's no chance that you and I can move this."

"It's empty and it looks heavier than it is."

He grimaced. "Are you really going to make me do this?"

"Hey, you're the one who volunteered for moving duty."

He heaved a sigh but tested the weight by tipping it forward. "Maybe on both dollies the way we did the couches," he said. "But where is it going?"

"My room."

Again he looked dubious. "I'd point out that your room is already full but I know it wouldn't do me any good. And have you taken the stairs into consideration? The landing at the top is not all that wide—what if we get it up there and can't turn the corner to the bedroom?"

"How about if I go for Chinese food for dinner and you measure things while I'm gone?" she suggested, hoping both bribery and enthusiasm would win the day. "The stairs won't seem nearly as daunting if we eat and rest a little first."

He dropped his head back and looked at the darkening sky as if for heavenly help. Then he conceded. "I like egg rolls."

She grinned. "I'll only be a few minutes."

It took her half an hour. Gabe was sitting on the front steps with another beer in hand when she got back. He looked as if he'd gone home and cleaned up; his hair was combed and the shadow of his beard that had developed as the day wore on was gone. Gracie appreciated the sight without comment.

They ate sitting on the lawn to catch the breeze, having to taste what was in each container in order to tell what it was because the only illumination came from the single bulb in the porch light.

When they were finished they ate their fortune cookies and squinted to read the proverbs inside. Then Gabe fell back into the grass, spread-eagle.

"Stopping at this point is deadly. I don't know if I can get up and go again," he said to the sky.

Gracie pulled a long blade of grass and ran the tip of it lightly along the underside of his outstretched arm.

He turned his head and opened just one eye to glare at her. "Is that supposed to entice me back to my feet?"

"No, it's supposed to torment you back to them."

"You'll have more success with enticement." He reached that same arm up to clasp his hand around the back of her head, pulling her down to kiss him.

His mouth opened under hers as if they were old hands at this. He tasted slightly of fortune cookie and smelled of after-shave and it took Gracie only a split second to open her own mouth almost as wide as his.

While his tongue teased hers, he let his palm slide down to her back, holding her with a gentle pressure. He took her hand with his free one and brought it to the center of his chest, rubbing feathery strokes along the underside of her wrist in a way that sent goose bumps all the way up both of her arms.

But after a few moments Gracie ended the kiss. "Are you trying to distract me so you don't have to move that armoire?" she asked in a quiet voice, her face not far above his.

He laughed, a deep, delicious sound, different than any she'd heard from him before. Better. More intimate. And just a shade devilish. "I guess it didn't work, is that what you're telling me?"

"You got it, Duran. On your feet and back to work."

She stood up and he clamped his hand around her ankle. "Adeline didn't tell me what a hard woman you are," he groaned. Then he got to his feet. "While you throw the dinner mess away I'll strap the armoire to the dollies."

"Great idea," she agreed with a satisfied smile, much too tempted to swat his rear end when he turned and headed for the garage. Maybe she was a dirty old lady.

The armoire was only slightly less difficult to move than the sofas had been, but the sofas hadn't had to go up a full flight of stairs. With Gracie on the bottom Gabe backed his way up, bearing most of the weight while she kept her shoulder to the antique and pushed.

Rounding the corner on the landing was no easy task but they made it, leaving the carved oak piece in the hall while Gracie tried to figure out where to put it.

"Let me guess," he said when she had studied the bedroom awhile. "You don't think it'll fit and we have to take it back down those stairs."

She shook her head. "It'll fit. But only if we move the bed to that far wall and put the TV in the corner."

"Anything is better than the stairs."

They rearranged the room, moving the bed out of the position it would end up in so that the armoire could pass it. Then they had to finesse the bed into the only spot it could take up.

With Gracie at the top corner and Gabe at the bottom corner of the opposite side, they pushed it a few inches at a time—first the head, then the foot, then the head again, until they had managed to turn it.

Gracie went to stand at the bottom and judge. "A little more your way, I think," she said.

Gabe took a step backward as she returned to her side and shoved.

"I know that was too much."

He bent over and pushed in her direction until the bed came up against her knees. For some reason Gracie didn't understand she had a heightened awareness of the feel of that mattress on her bare skin.

She ignored it and went to the footboard once more. "Now it's too far my way. We need it centered right underneath that fanlight window."

Back again she pushed from her side but the bed wouldn't move. She glanced up to find Gabe blocking it, an ornery smile on his face.

Feeling a little ornery herself, Gracie shoved so the bed bounced against him. "Move it, Duran."

He kneed the bed back at her. "Move what, Canon?" he asked in a more sensual tone, smiling archly.

By now they were standing face-to-face, their bare legs against opposite sides of the mattress. She pushed just enough for it to nudge him. "Move your knobby knees out of my way."

He nudged her back, holding it against her with one thigh this time, while he placed his other knee on the bed, leaning well over it, both hands flat on the mattress. "Did you really want to make another crack about my knees?"

"Funniest-looking things I've ever seen." She pulsed against the mattress just for effect.

"Is that right?" he said. Then he lunged for her before she could get away and pulled her down on the bed, pinning her there with his hands at her shoulders. "Looks like your punishment is going to have to be more severe this time."

She stuck out her tongue at him.

"Ooo, you're asking for it."

And he gave it, tickling her unmercifully until Gracie was writhing on the bed in giggling agony. "No fair, no fair."

He let up the slightest little bit and she seized the moment, rolling off the bed and heading for the doorway. But he was closer and beat her to it, blocking it with his hands on either side of the uppermost corners of the jamb.

Gracie had to grin. He'd left himself wide open to attack. She bobbed to the right and then to the left as if looking for a way around him. Just when he was intent on defending his goal she made a surprise assault with some heavy tickling of her own until she could get him out into the hallway enough to make a mad dash down the stairs.

"You're mine now," he called from behind her, his recovery too quick and his legs too long.

Gracie made it to the entryway, but he was close enough behind her to reach over the banister and catch her arm, pulling her back against him. "Gotcha."

"Okay, I give up. I'll never say another word about your knees."

Gabe sank down to the second step, pulling Gracie to sit on the first one in the V of his spread thighs. He still kept her captive with his arms wrapped around her and she willingly leaned back against him while she caught her breath.

Moments later, she dropped her head onto one of his knees and closed her eyes. The hair on his leg was prickly against her cheek but she liked it. "I'm beat."

He kissed the side of her neck, just below her earlobe, all the while running feather strokes up and down her arms. "Want me to carry you upstairs and put you to bed?"

She'd never admit just how good that sounded. "No, I've worked you enough for one day. I wouldn't want the movers' union on my case."

He massaged her shoulders then—deep, kneading pressure against her tired muscles. The feel of his big hands was soothing and exciting at once, and a soft groan escaped Gracie's throat.

She heard him laugh almost as softly and then he kissed his way down her neck to where it dipped into her shoulder. She felt the hot flick of his tongue there, lighting tiny sparks in that spot. It made her smile, her eyes still closed. "Oh, that's nice."

Somehow her hands had gone from dangling in space to clasp around his shins, and now they did some rubbing of their own, gently up and down. His skin was warm and taut.

He pulled her more firmly back into the lee of his legs, angling her on the lower step so he could tip her face up to him and reach her lips with his own, his palm along her jawbone holding her to his kiss. His mouth was wide open over hers, his tongue conveying an urgency, a hunger. Gracie was surprised by the power of those same answering needs in her.

She turned completely sideways on the step, reaching an arm around his waist and feeling the straining muscles of his back as he arched over her. His shirt had pulled up and somehow it seemed only natural to quench the thirst she had for slipping underneath to feel his skin there.

His hands were clasped around her far shoulder and she felt him slide one of them up her collarbone and then down just enough to let her know where he was headed before he paused as if waiting for her to stop him.

But how could she, when her breasts strained against the tight leotard for his touch?

After what seemed like much, much too long, he cupped her breast, but it was agony not to feel his hand against her bare skin, against her hardened nipple. Gabe must have sensed it, or maybe the barrier bothered him, too, because he didn't waste any time slipping the leotard strap down.

At the first brush of his palm to her exposed nipple it tightened up so hard and fast it nearly pinched. But his touch was just what she needed and Gracie couldn't keep from arching up into his hand.

One of his thick thighs braced her back and made a pillow for her head as Gabe went on plundering her mouth with his tongue. Gracie reached for the thigh that was in front of her. Without thinking about it she kneaded his leg as he did her breast.

Against her side she could feel the long thick ridge of his desire for her and she leaned in closer still. Too close for him to go on kissing her. He breathed an almost tortured breath as he released her mouth, pulsing against her just once before lifting her to sit in his lap.

His mouth found her breast then. Warm and wet, he drew her deeply inside, flicking her nipple with the very tip of his tongue.

Gracie's head fell back and she clasped his nape where his coarse hair met his neck, holding him to the wonders he was performing for her. It was as if each draw of her breast into his mouth tightened a cord that ran a straight shot to that spot between her legs that ached with need.

But then, in some leap from the sensual and emotional to the intellectual, she realized where this was headed, and remembered too well her earlier feelings of panic at that very thought. That panic was nothing more than a memory now. She could easily let him carry her to the bed upstairs and all too willingly make love with him. But would she be sorry for it afterward? Would she feel embarrassed? Was this only passion and hormones ruling now?

She couldn't take the chance.

For one more all-too-brief moment she indulged herself in the glory of his hands and mouth on her, in the bliss of feeling his engorged flesh against her hip, the rolling strength in the muscles of his back beneath her palms. And then she lifted his face upward for one last kiss—hungry and wanting—before she stopped him.

"I don't know if I'm ready for more," she said in a throaty whisper as he pressed another kiss where this had all begun, in the soft L of her neck and shoulder.

With his mouth still buried in that spot he pulled her leotard back in place. Then he straightened up and looked at her, smiling just slightly. "It's the knees, isn't it? They're too knobby. I've known rejection all my life because of them."

That made her laugh, instantly lightening the mood. Grateful for it, Gracie played along. "That's it. Have you ever considered plastic surgery?"

"Many times. But there's no help." He kissed her again. "Maybe you can find a way to overlook my knees if I wow you with my cooking? Say, tomorrow night?"

"I don't know. Are you inviting me for doggy stew?"

"I was thinking more along the lines of pasta primavera. My father tells me he has a new recipe that melts women's hearts."

Gracie thought her heart was already melting for this man. "Shall I bring wine?"

"No, just yourself. I'll take care of everything else."

"Sounds good."

He kept his arm around her, holding her close against his side as she walked him the last few feet to the front door.

"Thanks for all your help today and tonight," she said when he'd stopped and turned her to face him again, his arms riding low on her hips.

He nodded in the general direction of the upstairs bedroom. "Think you can get that bed into just the right spot without me?"

"I think I can manage."

"Tomorrow night at about seven, then?"

"I'll be there."

He kissed her once more, a slow, lingering thing that let her know it wouldn't take anything to light the fires between them again. With his mouth still on hers he took his arms away, holding them out at his sides for a moment before ending the kiss.

"I'm going now. Before it's too late."

He gave her one more quick kiss and then he was gone.

And Gracie wasn't at all sure that she'd made the right choice in seeing him to the door instead of letting him take her upstairs to bed.

Chapter Seven

Dean had already ordered for her when Gracie got to the small restaurant to join him for breakfast the next morning.

"Bacon and eggs, applesauce, orange juice and coffee, right?" he asked as she sat down.

"Right. I'm surprised you still remember. We haven't had breakfast together in probably a dozen years."

"And you're still eating the same thing."

She laughed. "Does that make me too predictable?"

"Lately, Gracie, predictable is the last thing I'd call you. I'm beginning to wonder if you're turning into the next Adeline."

"Who, me? I wasn't even tempted to wear one of our aunt's old baseball caps to breakfast this morning the way she would have."

"There's no comfort in that. She didn't start wearing those things until she noticed the bald spot she was getting. For all I know you'll do the same thing if and when you lose your hair."

"I was thinking more along the lines of English driving hats. Baseball was never the thrill for me that it was for Adeline."

Their meals arrived and while they were served neither of them said anything. But once the waitress left, Dean changed the subject.

"Did you turn up any of Adeline's friends who knew if she intended to sell the comic books?"

Gracie shook her head while she finished chewing her first bite of breakfast. "I called every single person in her address book and not one of them knew a thing."

Dean nodded as if that didn't surprise him. "I had dinner last night with the comic-book dealer—her name is Brandy."

"I thought she was a he?"

"So did I. But, believe me, we were both way off the mark."

"Ah, I see," Gracie said. "I take it you liked this person."

Dean shrugged as if the comic-book dealer didn't matter to him one way or another. "Her name is Brandy. She seems very nice. In fact, we had an appointment at three in the afternoon and she was so interesting that it carried over into dinner."

Gracie had to smile at her brother's caution not to seem too enthusiastic over a woman he had obviously found attractive. "Are you seeing her again?"

"Tonight. We're going to the movies," he said as if he were walking through hot coals.

"I hope you aren't letting her know how leery you are of women and relationships."

"It's okay. She's been through as much of the single scene as I have and she's the same way."

Gracie took a sip of her orange juice to hide a smile. She had an image of her brother and this woman as two timid puppies circling each other. "So which of you had the courage to suggest dinner last night and the movies tonight?"

"I offered to buy her dinner when we were still talking at seven last night and she wouldn't let me pay for her time or expertise. She suggested the movies tonight to repay me for dinner."

"What happens when you run out of excuses?" Gracie asked without being able to keep her amusement to herself any longer.

"It isn't funny, Gracie. I know you don't believe me when I tell you how rough it is to be single but I'm not exaggerating. And I'm worried that you're about to learn the hard way."

He made that last sound very ominous and she knew he was thinking about Gabe. Then he confirmed it.

"And I don't want your neighbor to be the one to teach you."

Gabe had already taught her a lot. How to feel good again, how to enjoy the company of a man again, a man's kiss, his touch. All good things. "He's a nice guy, Dean. You don't have to worry."

"He's a nice guy who wants you to sell him something you probably aren't supposed to sell him."

Gracie ignored the comment. "Tell me what Brandy said about the comics."

It was clear Dean wanted more of a debate on Gabe's merits and demerits, but he refrained. "When I told Brandy about the Baby Jack Flash comics she lit up like a firecracker. She said that there are several of the later issues in prime condition known to exist but only a few of those first three that you have. She was very concerned with how they'd been stored all these years and what kind of wear and tear they'd suffered. When I said they'd been in an old cedar box she was ecstatic—something about the atmosphere being acid free."

Dean stopped talking while his coffee cup was replenished. "Do you know if they've been graded—that's comic-book terminology for rating their condition?" he asked when the waitress left.

"Gabe didn't mention anything about it. Why?"

"Because that's the most important thing. No matter how old or rare a comic, if it's in bad shape it isn't worth much. I explained to her that these three looked new to me. Brandy—and apparently any number of comic-book collectors—would kill to get their hands on them."

"I hope you let her know that they'll be sold to Gabe or no one. I wouldn't want you to lead her on."

"I wouldn't do that," he said as if she'd injured him.

"Good, because the last thing I need is a fledgling relationship of yours hanging on these comic books, too," she teased.

"It isn't a relationship, fledgling or otherwise," he said. Then he went on relaying what he'd learned. "There are all kinds of things that come into play when a dealer grades comics. They even check the staples, believe it or not, to make sure they're the originals and that not so much as a chip of ink is missing around one. And there's something about some kind of coupons—whether or not they've been cut out. Anyway, she said they should definitely be graded before you agree to anything, because if these comics are truly in mint condition, they could be worth a lot more than that nice-guy neighbor claims Adeline agreed to sell them for."

"Gabe hasn't hidden what a coup it would be for him to handle these comics," Gracie pointed out as she took a bite of applesauce, trying not to dwell on the fact that every time her brother said the word *claim* he made it sound like a felony. "Who grades comic books? Are there people who specialize in it, like house appraisers?"

He shook his head as he finished chewing and swallowing a bite of bacon. "Any dealer can do it, but sometimes they disagree. Brandy has a reputation for being good at it."

"Then maybe Gabe graded them himself," Gracie suggested.

"Adeline would have been a fool to accept an appraisal from the person she was selling to."

"She wasn't selling the comics *to* Gabe. She was selling them *through* him. And as a dealer himself, I'm sure he's qualified to grade them and decide on a price."

"Qualified or not, he has too much at stake to be trusted."

"That isn't true. It's possible for a trustworthy person to still be a trustworthy person, no matter what the stakes."

"It's also possible that this guy is conning you."

Gracie finished her breakfast and pushed the dish away. "If Gabe was conning me why wouldn't he have persuaded his father to confirm Adeline's intentions to sell?" she asked, seizing something that had recently occurred to her. "It would have been the perfect backup, an ace in the hole. Eli is the person our aunt was most likely to tell, so no one would doubt his word, and Gabe could have saved himself all this grief."

"Maybe Eli wouldn't be a party to it. In fact, maybe the old man was trying to warn you when his son was out of the room the other morning and he said he didn't blame you for doubting this whole story because even he couldn't believe Adeline had been willing to sell anything."

"I definitely did not have the impression that Eli was trying to relay a subtle warning," she said forcefully, because it was true. What she kept to herself was the fact that the older man's doubts did have an annoying way of repeatedly popping up in her thoughts like a red flag.

"All right," Dean went on. "Then let's assume Eli genuinely knew nothing about this until after Adeline left, that he's only heard the same tale his son is telling you and doesn't have any better idea than you do about whether or not it's the truth. Isn't it possible that Duran knew ahead of time that his father would never conspire in something like this? That he concocted the whole story about keeping his financial problems from Eli just to cover his tracks because he knew his father was the person most likely to know about anything Adeline was doing?"

"Yes, it's possible," Gracie conceded. "But it's not any more possible than that Gabe might be telling the absolute truth and he's just been caught up in a stroke of bad luck and a poor postal system."

The waitress removed their plates and left the bill, which Dean immediately picked up. "Will you at least let Brandy take a look at the comics so she can grade them and tell you if the price is fair? There's no harm in that, is there?"

"No, I suppose not." Though Gracie was uncomfortable going along with what Dean seemed to think would strike one more blow against Gabe's credibility. She felt as if she was conspiring against him.

"That's my girl," Dean said as if he'd won a victory for truth, justice and the American way. "I'll set it up with her for as soon as possible."

Gracie left the tip and they went outside to the parking lot.

"What do you have planned for the rest of the day?" her brother asked at her car. "If you're free this afternoon I have an icebox I need you to check out to see if it's beyond repair."

"I can't today, Dean. Willy is coming over to help me work in the attic so I can move some things up there. Gabe spent all of yesterday carting my furniture in from the garage, so now I have to make up my mind what to use and what to store."

"Need more help?"

"Thanks, but I don't think so." She also didn't think she wanted to listen to more of her brother's suspicions about Gabe. She knew Dean's intentions were good and protective, but she didn't like to dwell on the negative when she was still hoping to find someone who would confirm Gabe's arrangement with her aunt so this whole mess would end in the best way for everyone involved.

"I'll call as soon as I know when Brandy can look at the comics," Dean went on. "In the meantime, be very careful with them. I didn't realize until talking to her how fragile they are, or how costly the slightest flaw can be." He hugged her. "And be careful with your nice-guy neighbor, too. You could still be pretty fragile, yourself."

Gracie had already started work on the attic when Willy arrived around noon. She'd left a note on the front door for her cousin so she didn't have to worry about not hearing the doorbell.

"What if somebody besides me saw that note and came in to ax-murder you?" was how Willy greeted Gracie as she climbed the last flight of steps.

"Axe murderers take Sunday off," Gracie answered from where she was kneeling on the attic floor surrounded by boxes. "Look what I found—some of Great-Grandma's and Adeline's old clothes. Remember how we used to want to try them on when we were kids?"

Willy came to stand beside her, putting one hand on her hip and pointing a single index finger nearly at Gracie's nose the way their aunt had, mimicking, "These are all I have left of my mother's things and they have better purposes than to entertain two ragtag little girls on a rainy day, I can tell you."

Gracie laughed out loud. "You sound just like her."

Willy dropped to her knees and pulled one of the boxes toward her. "Let's open them up and see what's inside."

Gracie was all too willing. She flipped up the top of another carton. What she found were lacy gowns wrapped lovingly in tissue. Taking one out as carefully as if it might crumble at her first touch, she stood up and held it in front of her. Time had turned the satin and lace the color of a tea stain, but the shape of the high neck and puffy sleeves was preserved with paper stuffings.

"These have to be from the turn of the century. Adeline was right—it would have been a shame for two kids to have gotten in and ruined them," Gracie said.

Willy fingered the lace of the overskirt that reached just above Gracie's ankles. "Isn't that gorgeous?" Then from her own box she unearthed a corset. "Except that they had to wear this underneath it," she said, making a face.

"Try it on," Gracie urged, setting her dress down so she could help her cousin with the boned bodice covered with shiny pink striped satin.

"It's a pretty torture chamber," Willy wheezed as if with her last breath.

"That's nothing. Look at these shoes," Gracie said, taking out leather boots with tiny pointed toes, high arches and ankles that buttoned up no bigger around than a good-size cucumber.

"It's a wonder they could walk," Willy agreed. "But get me out of this thing before I die."

Gracie obliged. Then they opened two more boxes. "These have to be Adeline's."

Willy pulled out a black satin number with a dropped waist. "Adeline was a flapper."

"Did you ever doubt it? She would have been—" Gracie calculated "—just hitting her twenties at the end of the era. Of course, she'd have been a part of it."

Gracie pulled out the dress that had been underneath the black satin. It had a tight waist, a big, full skirt and a strapless bodice that dated it considerably later. "How about this one? It looks like something out of an old movie."

"The fifties," Willy dubbed it, taking out of her box shoes with high, thick heels and the toes cut out.

"And gloves—you would have been in your glory, Wil," Gracie said as she opened a small quilted box filled with every different length imaginable.

"What are those? Big rubber bands?"

"Garters," Gracie amended as Willy pulled one out like a slingshot. They both tried them on, judging panty hose far superior.

Willy looked around at the mess they'd made. "Good job, Gracie. "You get me over here to help you clean things up and instead you make us make a bigger mess."

"It was worth it."

As they started to carefully replace the old clothes in their original boxes, Willy said, "Speaking of which, nothing was worth the phone calls I've made this week."

"About the comics?"

"If only that'd been all I had to talk about. Have you ever stopped to count how many cases of bunions and/or bursitis there are in our family?"

"No, how many?" Gracie laughed.

"Too many."

"Did anybody know about the comics?" Gracie asked as they stacked the clothes boxes against a wall.

"Not a single one of them even knew Adeline had comic books, let alone that she was thinking of selling them. In fact, there was a unanimous opinion that it was unlikely. Sorry, Gabe, old boy," she finished with a salute in the direction of the house across the street.

Finding the old clothes had lifted the glum mood Dean had left Gracie with this morning. But it came back now. "Are you sure you called everybody?"

"I called people, my mother called people, even my father called a couple of distant cousins that wouldn't have known anyone but him. It didn't matter whether they'd seen Adeline a year ago or the day she left, nobody knew what I was talking about."

Gracie didn't want to admit it, but suddenly her brother's suspicions felt a little less outrageous. "Damn."

"You know what Dean thinks about this," Willy said as if reading Gracie's mind.

"I had breakfast with him this morning. I find it hard to believe that this is some deep, dark plot on Gabe's part." Hard to believe? Before, she'd said she *didn't* believe it—unequivocally. But now, she realized, she couldn't say that because it wasn't true.

"You're probably right," Willy agreed. "Gabe Duran is too cute to be the hatcher of deep, dark plots."

"Really, the only thing proven by no one else knowing is that Adeline could keep a confidence, and we already knew that," Gracie went on, feeling a little better when she heard her own words.

"Does that mean you're going to sell the comics to him anyway, then?"

"I don't know." And she honestly didn't.

A part of her just plain couldn't believe Gabe was lying. But an equally strong part reminded her that her aunt had been almost phobically against selling her belongings and had trusted Gracie not to sell anything, either. Without confirmation that Adeline had felt differently about the comic books, how could she go through with the sale?

As Gabe cleaned vegetables for the pasta primavera he was preparing for dinner, he had a lot on his mind.

His father had abandoned Dave early at The Collector's Exchange the day before and left a cryptic message on Gabe's machine that he had a pressing engagement that required him not to finish work and would keep him from their walk this morning, and for the rest of the week, too.

Gabe didn't care about Eli leaving the shop; Dave had managed without him. And he didn't care about Eli missing their walks.

What he did care about was the reason behind everything.

Gabe and Murf had walked without Eli, and as they'd rounded the corner a block from home, there was Eli, in a bathrobe, sitting on the side porch having coffee with the woman they so often saw—the woman Eli had finally managed to meet in the grocery store—Marge.

Here we go again, Gabe had thought as Eli waved him up to the house. He'd figured his father had just launched a new romance. Instead, Eli had just launched a new marriage—compliments of a quick flight to and from Las Vegas the night before.

Didn't he ever learn? Gabe wondered as he cut broccoli. How many times was Eli going to meet, fall in love and marry women he barely knew?

"Seven times, as of now." Gabe answered his own question.

But this one was really bothering him. More than any of the other six had. Why was that?

Maybe because this most recent round made him realize that what was happening between him and Gracie fell into his father's pattern.

Not that anything seemed wrong with Gabe's feelings or his relationship with Gracie. On the contrary, everything seemed right. Perfect. In fact, nothing had ever felt so good before.

But all of his adult life he'd guarded against doing what his father had done with women. Against making the same mistake and not taking marriage and relationships seriously enough. For his own life he wanted one woman—one right woman—to settle down with, to have a family with.

He'd been careful in all of his relationships to take things slowly, not to let himself get carried away by a strong attraction, to really get to know a woman before even thinking about whether or not they might evolve into something serious.

Then he'd met Gracie and it was as if all those years of practice hadn't happened. He'd jumped in with both feet, gotten carried away by a strong attraction, and he was feeling very serious about her already. It seemed alarmingly like what happened with his father over and over again.

What if these feelings were what Eli felt each of those seven times the older man had married? What if his own feelings had no more staying power than Eli's had?

"How could this have happened when I've been so damn careful before?" he asked himself out loud.

But it had happened. He was falling in love with Gracie. He wanted her so much it was a raw hunger inside him. Every minute he spent away from her seemed like wasted time. Every minute he was with her passed too quickly. Even his bed—in which she had never been—felt empty without her.

Murf nudged his leg just then. Gabe gave the big dog a broccoli floret and said, "So what am I going to do?"

What could he do? He certainly wasn't going to stop seeing Gracie and end the relationship because it had some of the earmarks of those his father rolled in and out of. Maybe it was enough that he was aware of the similarities. At least he could look for warning signs—in himself, in Gracie, in their relationship—that might tell him one way or another if what they had together had the same impermanence as those many marriages of his father, the same flash-in-the-pan quality.

God, how he hoped for good signs.

Because one thing was absolutely out of the question: that Gabe could stop what was happening with Gracie.

* * *

A steamy soak in a sea of bubbles had a sensuality all its own, Gracie thought as she did just that late in the afternoon. She leaned her head to the back of the tub and closed her eyes. It didn't take more than that to bring Gabe's image to mind and her thoughts turned to the way the previous night had ended. Would she have been sorry if they'd made love?

She waited for the panic to come over her the way it had when she'd considered this possibility before. But it didn't, and she wondered why.

There were a few reasons, she guessed. One was the speed with which their relationship had grown right from the start. In keeping with that, spending the entire day and evening with him moving furniture had taken her feeling of familiarity another giant step forward. It was as if she'd known him all her life instead of just a short time.

But more than feeling comfortable with him, she cared about him in a way she recognized without much trouble. It was the same way she'd felt about Burt.

And when he'd kissed her the sparks that that kiss had ignited had fast turned into flames. Flames that seemed natural, and certainly too wonderful to resist. Fear of clothes coming off? At the moment when they had, the only thing on Gracie's mind had been good riddance.

No, she wouldn't have regretted it today if they'd made love last night.

"I'm sorry, Burt," she said out loud. But for the first time since her husband's death she finally felt as if she'd let him go.

As if it really was time to move on as a separate person.

* * *

"It smells wonderful," Gracie said when Gabe ushered her into his house an hour later.

"*You* smell wonderful," he said, leaning very near and breathing deeply.

She was a touch overdressed, Gracie realized as she took in his jeans and V-neck T-shirt, to her white slacks and spaghetti-strapped top. But maybe the bearer of bad tidings should hope her clothes proved a distraction.

"I have something to tell you and I think I better do it right off in case it changes your mind about feeding me." And she wanted to get it over with.

"That sounds pretty bad," he said as he flipped a dish towel over one broad shoulder and took her hand to bring her to the kitchen with him.

He turned the heat up on a pot of water, poured two glasses of wine and handed one to her. "Okay, let's hear it."

Gracie sipped the wine, buying herself a moment before she blurted out the whole thing. "I saw Willy today and between the two of us we can't find a single relation or friend who knows anything about the comics."

Gabe had been about to pour a dash of olive oil into the water but that stopped him. For a moment he just stared at the bottle in his hand and, as if she could read it in his expression, Gracie knew he was thinking about the lawsuit against him and losing his business. "That's pretty bad, all right," he said without looking at her, finally adding the oil to the water. "Are you telling me you won't go through with the sale?"

"No, there's still Adeline's lawyer. He'll be back from his vacation this week."

"One last hope."

Gracie wasn't sure whether she should apologize or keep a positive attitude. "One hope is better than none."

He didn't say anything for another moment. Then he seemed to rise above the worry that pulled his bushy brows together. He lifted his wineglass and clicked it against hers. "Here's to last hopes, then."

When they'd both sipped the wine he added the pasta to the now boiling water and took Gracie to the dining room where the ultramodern table was set with black plates and silverware that looked as if it were a souvenir from a space mission.

"I have some news," he offered when they sat down.

"Better than mine, I hope."

He chuckled wryly. "I'm not sure. My father dashed off to Las Vegas last night and got married again."

Gracie was glad for the change of subject, but even if she hadn't been she'd have wanted to hear about this. "The last letter from my aunt said he was swearing off marriage after six failed attempts."

"No, that's what a rational, reasonable man might do. But just like all the others, he met a woman he liked and the way other people have a second date, he got married." The timer went off in the kitchen and Gabe stood. "That means the macaroni is cooked. Stay where you are. I'll be right back."

Good to his word, he returned shortly with a salad bowl in one hand and a platter in the other.

"I take it you don't approve of your father's marriages?" she said as he served her pasta covered in a white sauce laden with broccoli, zucchini, snow peas and red and yellow peppers.

"I don't mean to say anything against him—my father is a great guy—but he never really has marriages. It's more like weddings are his hobby. Then, when the bloom wears off, he's out the door. No, I don't approve of it.''

''Does that have anything to do with you never marrying?'' she asked as he sat around the corner from her and filled his own plate. .

''It has a lot to do with it.'' He pointed his fork at her food as she took her second bite. ''How is my rookie effort at pasta primavera?''

''You could open a restaurant with it,'' she answered honestly.

The compliment obviously pleased him and for a moment Gracie was lost in the creases his smile left around his eyes and his mouth.

''Adeline used to give warnings against letting my father's adventures in matrimony affect me,'' he went on then. ''She'd say that I shouldn't let his track record sway me against finding a woman and settling down. That I had every chance of being as happy as you and your husband were. She was very proud of your successful marriage.''

One taste of his salad dressing was enough to pucker Gracie for a week, so she avoided any more. Before she could catch her breath from vinegar overdose he went on.

''Were you as blissful as your aunt thought?''

Gracie shrugged. ''I don't know how blissful she thought we were.''

''She said you were like two peas in a pod.''

''We were. We had the same taste in nearly everything from books to movies to food to furniture to fun. I guess we were just about inseparable.''

Gabe caught her eyes with his. ''I have a lot to compete against.''

Funny, but she hadn't thought about that. She hadn't been comparing the two of them. But, of course, now she did.

Gabe's hair had that slightly mussed look to it—so different from Burt's always impeccably combed style. But she liked his every bit as much as she had Burt's.

Gabe was taller and more muscular, but she only found that appealing and very sexy, without thinking less of Burt's more wiry physique. Gabe's voice was deeper and yet somehow quieter, and it managed to slide over her nerve endings like honey, not better or worse than Burt's, just nice all on its own.

In fact, the two men couldn't be more different, now that she thought about it. And yet that didn't change the feeling of warmth that seemed to wrap around her every time Gabe leveled those incredible blue eyes on her, or the shivers that went off in her when he smiled. It didn't change that one touch of those big hands of his could make her forget her own name, or that the smell of his much milder, airy scent of after-shave could make her light-headed.

"There's no competition. Burt was one person and you're another," she said softly, surprised to hear the breathy timbre of her own voice.

Gabe's smile was slow and lazy, nothing like Burt's quick grin, but just as welcome, just as endearing, maybe more enticing.

He nodded toward her plate. "You're not eating. Did I give you too much?"

Gracie tore her eyes away from his face to glance down at her food, realizing that there was an altogether different hunger in her that pasta would never be able to soothe. "Would I hurt your feelings if I said yes?"

He shook his head. "This is rich stuff. I can't finish mine, either." He stood and came around to pull her chair out. "It just occurred to me that I've never given you the grand tour of the rest of the house. Would you like to see it?"

"Sure," she answered. "I've been wondering where the holodeck is."

"As in spaceship? Is that a crack about my interior decorating again?"

Gracie just grinned and let him lead the way.

There was a small bedroom that held only exercise equipment, and Gracie realized to what his muscles could be attributed. Another slightly larger bedroom contained only a pool table in the center and several framed sports posters along the walls. And then there was his room.

It was not large for a master bedroom and the only item of furniture it contained was a king-size bed that stood nearly three feet high.

"Is that a water bed?"

"It is."

"Up on blocks?" she joked.

"The base is called an underdresser. There wasn't enough space for the bed and any kind of bureau, too, so I have twelve drawers in the base of the bed."

"And you need a ladder to get into it." Gracie couldn't resist going over and pushing down on the black quilt that covered the mattress.

"Have you ever slept on a water bed?"

Was that a proposition? No, it just sounded as if he was asking a simple question. "Never."

"You don't know what you're missing. Lie down on it and see what it's like." Then, at her hesitation, he leaned a shoulder against the far wall and crossed his arms over his chest. "I promise I'll stay all the way over here."

She felt a little silly, but Gracie was dying to try the bed, so she turned her back to it, hiked herself onto the padded leather side rail, and swung onto the mattress.

The water rolled away from her and for a moment she had the feeling that she was going to fall. But then the water came back in a wave that lifted her slightly before it settled down.

Little by little, not trusting it, Gracie stretched out flat, her head on the pillow, her arms at her sides, palms against the quilt.

"Relax," Gabe advised with a laugh.

The bed finally stopped swaying and molded around the contours of her body much like her feather bed did at home. "It's nice," she decided, giving a tiny bounce to make the water beneath her roll again just for fun.

Gabe didn't say anything and when she glanced at him she found him watching her with a new intensity in his smoky blue eyes. She had the strong sense that he was joining her on the bed in his mind, if not in actuality, and it was as if that image conveyed itself to her thoughts with a sudden vivid flash.

The urge to invite him to join her, to ask him to lie beside her, hold her, kiss her, make love to her, was as strong as a tidal wave.

Gracie bolted to a sitting position and swung out of the bed as if it had just caught fire. The first thing to catch her eye as she did so was the sliding glass door that opened the bedroom to a small terrace where a huge telescope stood.

Gratitude for the diversion pushed her outside. "You're a stargazer? Or do you use this to spot spaceships you can hijack for new furniture?"

A glance over her shoulder found Gabe still staring at that bed for a moment as if what he was seeing there continued to hold him transfixed. Then, very slowly, he seemed to pull his gaze away and focus on her. "It's a good telescope but not quite good enough to spot space-ships."

He followed her out onto the terrace, where Gracie studied the telescope itself. The tripod was stained cherrywood, and the telescope, mounting, clamp, cradle and control knobs were all polished brass. "An eighteenth-century English mariner's telescope," she dubbed it, admiring the impressive instrument.

"A reproduction," Gabe amended.

"I would have figured you for one that looked like something that came out of the twenty-first century."

He stood close beside her, adjusting the telescope so she could see through it. "It may look old-fashioned, but the optics and resolution are state-of-the-art. I bought it for what I can see through it, not for how it looks."

"Well, it's beautiful, just the same."

Gabe came to stand behind her, raising the eyepiece another notch. She leaned into it, seeing diamond-chip stars in the clear black sky. But then she felt his hands on both of her shoulders and her appreciation turned inward to the skitter of diamond chips that exploded from his touch.

He was telling her she was looking at Orion's belt but Gracie couldn't have picked it out if there were arrows pointing to it. "Amazing," she said, and although she was breathing a sigh over the effects of his nearness and a slight touch of his hands, it was just as well that he believed she was referring to the stars.

Gracie straightened from the telescope then, finding that was all it took to come up against Gabe. "I'm impressed," she said again, willing him not to take his hands away.

He didn't. Instead, as if the stirrings in her own body had made themselves known to him, he moved her hair away from the side of her neck with his thumb and pressed a kiss there. Softly. Sweetly.

Gracie turned her head and tilted it enough to expose even more of her skin to him. His breath there was warm; his body running the length of hers from behind was big and powerful, and cupped hers as gloriously as his water bed had a few minutes before.

A wave of tension rippled through her. Should she go back to pretending an interest in astronomy?

His hands slipped down her arms and left a trail of goose bumps in their wake.

Now was the time to stop anything from getting started, she realized.

But she didn't want to stop it. In fact, after the frustration of the night before, she was eager for more.

She crossed her arms so that she could reach a hand to cover each of his, and pressed her back more firmly into the sheltering cove of his chest, laying her head against his shoulder. She swallowed a small wave of tension and closed her eyes, giving in to the sensations of her body.

"I've been worried today that I rushed you last night," he said into her shoulder, his voice a midnight timbre. "I don't want to do that."

"It wasn't you. I wasn't sure myself, last night," she answered in a husky whisper of her own.

He kissed his way to the edge of her shoulder, then turned her to face him. Gracie looked up into his handsome, moon-washed features. He held her head in his hands, closing out the rest of the world, centering her attention, her every sense, on him, on what she felt for him.

"I could very well be falling in love with you, Gracie. But I can wait for this if you're still not sure."

She smiled at him. Nothing in the world seemed more natural than to be there with him, in his arms. "I could very well be falling in love with you, too," she answered him.

"Still—"

She pressed her fingers to his lips. "I'm sure."

He kissed her fingertips and then brought her hand down to his chest, holding it there, pressed to his heart. He captured her mouth with his, open and demanding and hungry already, as if her consent was all it took to open the floodgates of his desire for her. And Gracie was eager to answer with her own parted lips and thrusting tongue.

He released her hand and wrapped his arms around her, pulling her up tight against him as if he'd just caught her and was afraid she'd get away.

But Gracie wasn't going anywhere. Instead, she held him as tightly, learning the rise and fall of the muscles in his broad back.

He broke away from their kiss. "You know I'm going to take you to bed?" he asked, slowly searching her eyes for confirmation that she understood what she was agreeing to, that this was no rash act.

She smiled her consent. "On the water bed?" she managed to joke.

"Definitely on the water bed," he answered, taking her back into the room.

The length of the leather side rail came up against their sides as he turned her into his arms again to kiss her less urgently, as if forcing himself to slow down for her.

"Relax and let me take care of everything," he whispered into her ear, nibbling a little of her lobe while he was at it.

Gracie was a long way from relaxed, but the tension wasn't a bad thing. It gave her a heightened awareness of his every touch, his every stroke.

She tugged with her teeth on his bottom lip and then his top one. Her hands were on his chest again and she found the edges of his V neckline to test the texture of the smattering of hair that had peeked out at her all evening. His skin was smooth and taut and when his mouth dropped to her shoulder once more she kissed him there, breathing deeply of the lingering scent of after-shave and him.

She felt him lower both of her straps and was suddenly glad she'd chosen a top that required her to go braless.

He kissed and nibbled his way down her arm, and each contact set off an explosion all its own so that she didn't even realize he'd unbuttoned the back of her blouse until it slipped down and he whisked it away.

He left her then, for only the split second it took to grab the bottom of his shirt in both hands and pull it over his head. He tossed it away and reached for her, pulling her so that her bare flesh met his, making him groan with that first exquisite contact. And when his mouth found hers again there was something different about it—more intimate, less urgent, slower and more sure. There was an expertise in this kiss, a savoring, that told her he was forgetting to be so careful with her. And she liked it.

He drew her upper lip into his mouth, teasing it with the tip of his tongue. Then he kissed her lightly before moving only far enough away to barely sever the contact, and trailed his tongue along the edges of her teeth.

Once more without her awareness of it, he'd unfastened the back button and zipper of her slacks and now they glided down to her ankles, her underwear along with them.

That gave Gracie a moment's pause. The sudden shock of being totally naked knocked a hole of self-doubt in her desire. But it lasted only long enough for Gabe to shed the rest of his clothes, because then she was too interested in the play of moonlight and shadow on his bare body to think of anything else.

Her imagination had not done him justice. He was much more masculinely beautiful in the buff, and as if her hands were drawn to him, Gracie reached out to run her palms up his biceps, over his shoulders and down to pectorals that were so hard they seemed flexed even when they weren't.

He whisked her up into his arms then and set her on the bed. The water rushed out from under her until he joined her and then she rode the crest of the wave his body made.

She opened her arms to him and in he came. The inside of his elbow arched around the top of her head so he could play with her hair while his other hand cupped her shoulder first and then worked its way down to her breast.

Finally!

Gracie lost a little burst of sound from her throat at his first touch, and she couldn't have stopped herself from arching into his palm even if she'd wanted to. Such big hands—kneading, rolling, learning what merely pleased and what drove her wild.

Then his mouth followed suit, sucking, gently nipping, circling, flicking. Wonderful shots of white lightning went off through her and brought her leg up over his hip before she even realized what she was doing.

Gabe made an approving sound and reached his now free hand to her rear end, introducing her more firmly to that long, thick hardness that spoke of a burgeoning need of his own.

And she wanted him, needed him, every bit as much. She pulsed against him to let him know.

With his hand still cupping her derriere he lifted her atop his inner thigh, pulled her leg a bit higher over his hip and, as if they were made for each other, slipped himself inside her.

Pleasure was a small moan in her throat as she felt the sleek length of him filling her completely, pressing up into the heart of her.

His arms went around her then, holding her against him, as that first deep plunge sent the waves of water rolling around their ebb and flow, matching each thrust and slight retreat in perfection.

Gracie rode along, until it was as if each wave washed all the way through her, taking her near the very tip of ecstasy again and again until she finally reached the crest and stayed for that long, blissful moment of explosion.

And then, just when Gracie remembered to breathe again, Gabe gave one last, vital thrust, holding her hips pressed so tightly against his that they seemed fused, before he relaxed again and let the water carry them back to earth.

After a while the bed settled and left them just lying together, entwined, joined, as comfortable as if they'd always been this way, with Gabe cradling the back of her head in one hand.

"Interesting item, a water bed," she managed with a soft laugh into his chest.

"Isn't it, though?" he agreed. He kissed the top of her head, sighing into her hair. "Tell me you feel as good at this moment as I do."

"How good is that?"

"Incredible."

"At least that good," she joked, but it was true, nevertheless.

"Now tell me you won't move an inch until tomorrow morning."

"Not even an inch?" She pulsed against him.

"Not even a millimeter." He pulsed back.

"Is that possible?"

"Let's try."

Gracie wriggled around a little before agreeing. "Okay."

He groaned. Then he kissed her again. "This is right, Gracie," he said as if he thought she might doubt it.

But she didn't. It felt right to her, too, something she'd thought she might never find again.

She basked in the feel of his hands rubbing her back, of his body cupped around hers, of his chest beneath her cheek. She could hear his heartbeat and his slow, steady breathing, and her own seemed in sync with them.

Then his hands stilled, resting against her skin, and she felt his muscles ease from around her just enough to let her know he'd fallen asleep.

And with a last goodbye to the past, she followed him.

Chapter Eight

Gracie dreamed she was floating on a raft. Lying on her back, she felt the sun warm her face and her naked breasts. Content and feeling wonderfully weighted, she thought she could drift along like this forever, Burt by her side, his big, sturdy leg riding the length of hers....

Burt? No, it couldn't be Burt.

She came awake with a jolt.

Burt was gone. But that leg most definitely belonged to a man.

And then she remembered. Of course, it was Gabe. And, of course, for a moment she'd thought it was Burt. This was the first time she'd ever awakened in bed with anyone else.

Silently apologizing to Gabe for even unconsciously mistaking him for her late husband, she pulled the covers up to her chin and turned to look at him. He slept on his back, one arm under his head, the other across his stomach, his face turned toward her.

His hair was tousled and his cheeks were shadowed with dark stubble that reminded her of her initial impression of him the night they'd met—ruggedly, slightly dangerously good-looking.

So. Here she was, in bed with a man who wasn't Burt.

Somehow it seemed as if it should feel more strange than it did.

But when she thought about it she realized that she was okay with what had happened between her and Gabe. Burt was gone and nothing could bring him back. Gabe was here, and somehow when she wasn't looking she'd fallen in love with him. And that was all right because what she'd had with Burt wasn't lessened any by her feelings for Gabe. Just as what she felt for Gabe wasn't shadowed by her memories of, or feelings for, her late husband.

With his eyes still closed, Gabe rolled to his side and put his arm across her rib cage. "Toasted bagels with honey."

"No, sorry. It's just me—Gracie."

That made him smile, a lazy, languid thing. "Better yet." He opened his eyes. "What's on your agenda today?"

"Conquering my kitchen. Now that I've condensed all of my aunt's things I need to put mine in the cupboard space I freed up."

"Sounds like good work for tomorrow."

"What sounds like good work for today?"

"Spending it with me. I'll make you the executive vice president of The Collector's Exchange."

"How's the pay?"

"Bagels for breakfast, take-out lunch and dinner, and me."

"An irresistible offer."

He kissed her temple. "Welcome to the firm." Then he stretched and headed for the side rail. "Stay where you are. Certain very important executive VPs get breakfast in bed."

He swung off the mattress, and Gracie rode the waves and watched. His muscular back was the first thing she got to see and then a brief glimpse of his oh-so-fine rear end just before he pulled his pants on. There was something very sexy about him zipping his jeans, something even sexier about the waistband snap left unfastened and the line of dark hair like a connecting rod from his navel downward.

He tossed her his T-shirt from the night before and the scent of his after-shave came with it. "I wouldn't mind bagels in the buff but if you have a moral objection you can slip into that while I'm gone." Then he nodded to a closed door on the bedroom's inside wall. "Bathroom's through there. I'll be back before you know it."

"When do I report for duty?"

"In about half an hour."

"Half an hour? You're kidding, right?"

"Nope. Do you think everybody keeps renovator's hours? I have a lease that dictates when my doors open."

"Skip the bagels for me, then. I have to go home and get ready."

"How long does it take?"

"Longer than half an hour. Now go away so I can get up."

"Would it do me any good to point out that you got to watch me get up?"

"Only to waste time."

"That's what I thought. Okay, I'll go toast you a bagel for the long walk home."

The Collector's Exchange occupied a space in the main section of one of Denver's largest shopping centers. The entire front opened directly onto the mall and there were no windows or back door.

"I set it up something like a newstand," Gabe explained as he flipped on the lights.

For a moment Gracie's gaze followed him, reveling in the sight of him in a bright red polo shirt and khaki pants. But then she turned her attention to his shop.

The counter and glass cases that displayed sports cards, coins and the accessories that went with collecting them took up an entire side wall. Across from that were magazine racks—one for collectors' periodicals and informational publications, the rest for comics that were particularly in demand.

At the very back of the store were tables with boxes on them, each box a different letter of the alphabet, where a customer could search through hundreds of comic books sealed in plastic. The walls were covered with old sports posters and framed samples of baseball cards, and a few of the more expensive comics hung from twine strung across the ceiling.

"This place looks like a boy's idea of heaven," Gracie said when she'd taken in the whole store.

"I can't speak for all boys, but it was my idea of heaven as a kid," he said with a note of pride in his voice. "Actually, it's my idea of heaven now—at least for a workplace."

"Where did you work before this?"

"In the oil industry. Suits and ties and office politics every day. I was glad to get out."

"And start The Collector's Exchange."

"I suppose it's the kid in me. But I wanted to do something with my days that I enjoyed. That I looked forward to when I got up in the morning. I was too old to become a golf pro and not likely to make it on the chess circuit. That left sports cards and comic books and old coins—my other hobbies."

"Does coming here make you happy to get up in the morning?"

"Absolutely." His grin confirmed it. "How about a cup of coffee?"

"Sounds good."

As he filled the pot and plugged it in, Gracie browsed. Everything was neat and orderly, and even though most of the contents of the place were used there was a feeling of newness to it all that spoke of loving care and attention to detail.

When she came across the periodicals she took a comic-book price guide off the rack and thumbed through it. There was information on how to store comics, how to handle them, terminology, advice on how to start a collection or how to trade once a collection existed. And there was an explanation on grading them that reminded Gracie of her breakfast the day before with Dean.

"Here you go," Gabe said as he joined her, handing her a mug. "What are you reading?"

"I'm learning everything I ever wanted to know about comic books."

"Such as?" he asked as he looked over her shoulder. Then he answered his own question. "Grading?"

"I didn't know there was a thing." Well, not before yesterday morning, anyway. "Who grades them?"

"I do. Anybody who sells them does. It's a relatively informal system."

"Isn't that confusing?"

"There are guidelines. Sometimes there are disagreements over a grading, but not often."

"Did you grade the Baby Jack Flash comics or had that been done before?"

Gabe laughed. "Adeline hadn't touched them since shortly after she bought them, let alone had them graded. I did it."

"Did they get an A plus?"

He pointed to the pages open in her hands. "It isn't that kind of a system. See, it ranges from pristine mint—which is absolutely perfect in every way, to mint and on down through fine and very good for those that show some wear. Poor means they're damaged or heavily read, and coverless explains itself, but either of those makes them no good for collection purposes."

"And the Baby Jack Flashes?"

"I gave them a pristine mint grading. I'm sure you've taken a look at them, haven't you? They're like new. The pages are even still white—a big plus."

"Is it standard practice for the person handling the sale to do the grading, too?" she asked, looking at the magazine in her hands rather than at him.

"Sure. Like I said, it's all pretty informal. If anybody has a problem with it they can always get an independent opinion."

Two boys came into the store then. Gabe seemed to know them, and left Gracie in order to say hello and help them make up their minds between two rookie football players' cards.

She replaced the magazine she'd been looking at, feeling appeased and vindicated for her defense of Gabe to her brother. The Baby Jack Flash comics couldn't get a better grading than Gabe had given them, so obviously he hadn't underrated them, as Dean seemed to suspect. It only followed that the price was top dollar, as well, so when Dean brought his lady expert she could confirm this, at least, to Dean.

Hopefully, Adeline's lawyer would confirm the agreement and this whole business could be laid to rest.

Putting the sale of her aunt's comic books out of her mind, Gracie turned to watch Gabe with his young customers. He was knowledgeable and informative, patiently answering all the boys' questions and giving them what sounded like good advice. And he seemed as enthusiastic as they did.

He really loves this, Gracie thought.

She imagined him in a three-piece suit, with a briefcase, taking charge of a meeting. And although she could form the image in her mind, she couldn't see him happy at it. Certainly she couldn't see him as enlivened as he was, enjoying it the way he was enjoying this.

When the boys left, Gabe set the cards they hadn't purchased back under the glass counter, straightening a few others while he was at it—even though they didn't seem to need straightening. It made Gracie laugh. "You told those boys everything on that shelf was two dollars and now you're putting them back as carefully as if they were worth two thousand."

Still reaching into the display case, he looked up at her from beneath his brows, smiling a little sheepishly. "Are you making fun of me, Canon?" he asked in a way that let her know he didn't mind.

Gracie went to sit at the counter on one of the tall stools that faced it. "Do you have collections of your own?"

"How could I resist? My comics probably couldn't be considered a collection. I own a few early issues but most of what I have are just what I bought as a kid. The coin collection I store in a safety deposit box. But the baseball cards I keep here in case I get the chance to show them off." He wiggled those bushy brows. "Do you want to see them?"

"Do I have a choice?" she teased, since he was already pulling out a wooden case from below the display cabinet.

Opening the case, he spread albums and separate cards on the counter as if they were baby pictures and he the proud papa. For close to an hour he regaled her with anecdotes of how and when and why he'd acquired each card, looking as if he couldn't believe it when Gracie didn't know one player from another, and again she realized how this excited him.

"What I don't understand," she said when he finally finished, "is how come someone with such an affinity to everything contemporary has such a fondness for a bunch of old cards, or comic books or coins?"

He laughed. "Beats me. How come someone with your affinity for everything old likes new appliances and high-tech tools?"

"Because they're more functional. You can't say that about these things, though. Maybe you'll just have to admit there's charm in what's seasoned."

"Never," he teased. "I think the cards and comics just hark back to childhood and that's what appeals to me. They're like having a piece of it to relive."

And he definitely got involved enough in them to relive it, she thought, realizing it endeared him to her all the more.

Just then two men from a delivery service arrived with several boxes. It took three trips to get everything into the shop and then Gabe signed a shipping form that acknowledged he'd received them.

"This is the inventory from the store across town that closed. Remember I told you about the owner retiring and referring me to the group of collectors who want the Baby Jack Flash comics? I'm handling his things on a consignment basis."

Gracie nodded, feeling a little ashamed of herself because once again, unbidden, she'd been wondering how and why he would have invested in so much stock if his business might be about to go under. "Can I help?" she asked, to make amends.

His blue eyes took in her navy slacks and white camp shirt. "You aren't dressed for lugging dirty boxes but everything is going to have to be logged and marked so I can keep track of what belongs to this other guy. If you leave the lifting to me you can definitely help with the rest."

"Oh, good. But can you save some of your he-man strength for later? I have a couple of things I need help getting up into the attic tonight when we leave here."

He clasped his arm around her neck and pulled her in for a playful hug. "For a minute you got my hopes up that you wanted me to save my strength for something else." Then he planted a loud kiss on her lips and they went to work.

From ten in the morning until nine at night was a long day. Gracie leaned her head against the back of Gabe's passenger seat and closed her eyes when they'd finally closed the shop and found his car in the mall parking lot.

Gabe got in behind the wheel. "You aren't calling it quits, are you? I thought you still wanted me to help you get a few things up into your attic," he said as he started the engine.

"I'm recharging."

He slid his hand between the back of her neck and the seat, massaging her nape, and Gracie had to smile. She wondered if he had any idea what his slightest touch did to her and just how far it went in that recharging she'd mentioned.

"If you're too beat I can come over earlier than everyone else tomorrow night and help you then," he said, referring to her invitation for the small dinner party she was having for Gabe, Willy, Dean, and Eli and his new wife.

Gracie shook her head without opening her eyes. "I need the stuff out of the way so I can spruce the place up tomorrow. By the time we get home I'll be ready to roll again."

They spent the drive in silence from then on, but even with her eyes closed Gracie had a strong awareness of Gabe beside her. His warmth seemed to reach out to her even when he wasn't touching her. Just his presence nearby filled her senses and made her feel the way she had with Burt—complete, safe, cared for.

Once the car was in Gabe's garage they went into his house to get Murf and bring him along with them to Gracie's.

As they crossed the street Gabe reached for her hand and pulled her to walk more closely beside him. "You know, I really only intended to have you keep me company when I suggested that you come to the shop with me this morning. But thanks for all your help today."

"You're welcome, but I owed you one for all that furniture moving you did on Saturday."

He grinned wickedly as Gracie put her key in the front door and opened it. "What do I get for furniture moving tonight?" he asked.

"What do you want?" she countered with a little smile at the insinuation in his tone.

"How about a back rub," he suggested, making it sound like something that involved more than rubbing his back.

"Just a plain, simple, run-of-the-mill back rub?" she qualified it, flipping on the entryway light as the three of them went inside.

"Sure, what else?"

Gracie laughed at his mock innocence as he followed her into the living room. She reached for the pull chain on the Tiffany lamp beside the couch but before she could use it he swung her around to face him. He locked his hands behind her back and let his forearms rest on her waist.

"After bending over those boxes all day long and then moving whatever it is you want me to move to the attic, I'll need a back rub," he explained. "A small price to pay for making me a beast of burden again."

"True," she mused, pretending to think about it.

"Is it a deal?" he asked, kissing her chin and sending little sparks of white light from that spot all the way through her.

"Deal," she agreed in a voice that had suddenly gone a little breathy. Then she pulled out of his arms and finally lit the lamps. When she turned back to Gabe he was glancing around the room.

"Amazing. You actually managed to fit most everything in."

"*Most* everything, but not all of it. A lot of things had to go into closets or to the cellar or the attic already. And I was hoping to be able to squeeze the sofa table and bench in somewhere, but I just can't."

"Still, it doesn't even look cluttered. I'm impressed." Then he pointed to two boxes of books on the coffee table. "Do these go up to the attic, too?"

"I can do those tomorrow on my own."

He piled one on top of the other and picked them both up "Doesn't that beep coming from the kitchen mean you have messages on your answering machine?"

"Yes."

"Then why don't you find out who called and I'll take these upstairs so they're out of our way before we do the furniture. I'm in a hurry for my back rub."

"Okay. You're the boss today."

It occurred to Gracie that her brother could have called and said something she might not want Gabe to hear, so she made her way slowly into the kitchen. Not until she heard Gabe's footsteps on the stairs did she press the play button.

The first call was from Dean, all right, telling her that Brandy had a few free minutes late the next afternoon to look at the comics. Hearing that, Gracie cast a guilty glance down the hallway to make sure Gabe hadn't come back soon enough to hear.

He hadn't.

The second call was from the secretary at Adeline's attorney's office informing Gracie that Mr. Treble had checked in and wanted her to know he'd be happy to talk to her the following day when he returned to work.

Gabe came to stand in the doorway just as the machine clicked off. "Ready?"

She nodded and followed him into the living room. As they got on opposite ends of the sofa table she related the attorney's message.

"I'll keep my fingers crossed," he said as they headed up the stairs with it, but he didn't seem to want to say any more on the subject and Gracie was just as happy to let it drop.

On the way back down Gabe kept his hands on her shoulders, teasing her about overworking him. But his words stopped short when they got to the living room and found the dog lying on the middle cushion of her couch.

"Murf! Get down," Gabe chastised the animal.

But the big dog looked so comfortable and raised his eyebrows with such an attitude of forlorn pleading that Gracie had to laugh. "It's okay. Let him stay," she said as she turned to the last piece to be moved.

The bench was about four feet long, with a padded tapestry-covered seat and curved Queen Anne mahogany legs. Faced with exiling it, Gracie had second thoughts. "Let's take it to the bedroom instead and see if putting it at the foot of the bed would leave enough space to walk. If not, I'll put it in the attic, but I hate to."

"You're hopeless," Gabe told her as he picked it up himself and climbed the stairs.

Placed at the foot of her massive bed, the bench left not more than two feet of walkway between it and the facing wall. Gracie traveled the path a few times to decide if she could live with that and then opted to leave it.

"Great," Gabe said. His arms formed an X over his stomach, and he grasped the bottom of his red polo shirt and peeled it off over his head. Then he fell face first onto the big feather tick.

"What do you think you're doing?" Gracie asked.

"Waiting for you to pay up on the back rub you owe me."

"Here?" she said as if the idea scandalized her, when she was really enjoying the sight of him on her bed.

"Of course, here. You may have done a good job downstairs merging your furniture with Adeline's but you didn't leave enough floor space for me to stretch out there. I'm too long for the couch, and a person has to be lying flat to get the true benefit of a back rub." He smiled over his shoulder at her. "Come on, I'm in need of your ministrations," he said just before resting his head on his crossed arms and closing his eyes.

For a moment Gracie stood at the foot of the bed, staring at him. Her gaze rode the swells and valleys of his broad shoulders and then followed the long, deep indentation of his spine to the taper of his narrow waist. His skin was taut and smooth and tanned.

She swallowed against the catch in her throat, felt her pulse speed up and couldn't resist climbing on her knees onto the bed. She straddled his backside and pressed the heels of her hands to the dip of his waist, raising them with infinite slowness up the ever-widening breadth of his rib cage to his shoulders.

"Oh, that's nice," he groaned, shifting his muscles under her hands as Gracie trailed all the way up onto the relaxed bulges of his biceps. Then she reversed the path and let her flattened palms mold themselves to every mound and muscle all the way down again.

She felt his derriere tighten and pulse up against the intimate junction of her legs, letting her know that what she was doing to him was causing more than a simple back rub might. And that was all it took to make that spot on her body come alive with a few ideas of its own.

She answered him with just the slightest downward roll of her hips.

"You're supposed to be relaxing," she told him, her voice soft and low but edged with a little laugh.

"What makes you think I'm not?" he returned in a husky tone.

She kneaded his sides. "You don't feel too pliable."

He chuckled. "I'm not. I'm hard all over. But that doesn't mean I'm not relaxed . . . in a way."

She curled her hands around his shoulders and felt his warm, furrowed skin between her fingers. The tendons along the sides of his neck were tight and she traced them with her thumbs all the way up to behind his ears.

This time when his derriere arched against her he rose farther and turned onto his side, reaching around her with one arm as he did to bring her flat on her back on the mattress beneath him.

"You have magic hands," he told her in a ragged whisper.

"It's a gift," she joked just before he took her breath away by clasping the back of the thigh that still wrapped his hip and pressing his front side to that sensitive spot that had ridden him a moment earlier.

"I'd like to give you something, too," he said with a devilish laugh, pulsing against her again and again to let her know what.

She couldn't help the soft moan that found its way out of her throat in response any more than she could stop from pressing her hips up into him. Not that she wanted to stop. What she wanted was him, and all the gifts he was inclined to give her.

His lips were parted and she saw him run the tip of his tongue along the inside of the lower one just a split second before he took her mouth with his. Wide open and hungry from the start, Gracie matched him, feeling the same urgency in herself that obviously propelled him.

While his tongue and hers played cat and mouse he unfastened her blouse with impatient fingers, slipping it and her bra off as if they'd never get out of his way and free her breasts to his hands. Wonderful, glorious hands that filled themselves with her oh-so-sensitive flesh, kneading, molding, sculpting her with a master's touch and making her nipples harden into his palms.

And then he found one breast with his mouth, circling the crest with the tip of his tongue, flicking it, nipping, sucking just enough to drive her wild.

Suddenly she realized her fingers were digging into his back and she dragged them around his sides to his own puckered nibs, giving him a taste of the delicious torture he'd given her.

He reached to slide her slacks and underwear down and out of his way, baring her to his seeking hand and probing fingers and making her forget everything else as her back arched into his mouth and grasp at once, her body screaming to feel more of him inside her.

"Gabe—" she pleaded.

He tore himself away with a groan of his own and when he came back the rest of his clothes were blessedly gone.

"Oh, Gracie," he said, the words dragged through a ragged throat as he cupped her breast in his hand to bring the very tip back into his mouth before reaching below again to drive her more insane than she'd ever been before.

But she had to have more of him. She pressed a firm path with her palm down from his chest to his muscled stomach and then lower, finding the sleek, satiny hardness of him. She felt him tense at that first touch of her hand and then he flexed his hips even farther into her hold, forcing her to tighten her fist around him.

And then he came over her, into her, in one lithe movement, pulling both of her legs around his waist as his mouth again found hers. He slipped himself deeper and deeper inside her until she had all of him embedded and filling that void that needed him so desperately.

A small, high-pitched sound echoed in her throat as he began to move, flexing in, pulling out, in and out, slowly at first, each thrust a divine agony, each release creating a fiercer hunger, a greater need in her until she was moving, too, meeting him and drawing back, only to meet again.

Faster and faster he went then, until she couldn't keep up, until she didn't have to as each thrust drove him home. She could only hold tight to him as they climbed and climbed, higher and higher, until one splendid surge shot them both onto a simultaneous peak that seemed to fuse them, body and soul.

His movements slowed above her, inside her, and Gracie let him take her by lazy degrees back to earth. She heard him release a long sigh, and muscle by muscle he eased the warm blanket of his weight onto her.

He smoothed her hair from her damp forehead and kissed her. "I have the feeling—" and there he pulsed inside her "—that we were made for each other."

It certainly seemed like the right fit to her, so she pulsed back and said only, "Mmm," in agreement.

For a moment more he stayed there, and then he slipped from her and was gone—off the bed, out of the room.

"Don't go anywhere," he ordered from somewhere down the hall.

As if I could, she thought, feeling as if her body were a lead weight sunk into the feather mattress. She closed her eyes and let herself drift.

The next thing she knew she heard the water turned on in the bathtub and Gabe was back. He stood beside the bed, gloriously naked in the indigo light of the Tiffany lamp on the night table.

Without saying a word, he swept her up into his arms and carried her to the bathroom, where a dozen candles set on the floor around the claw-foot bathtub cast a buttery glow that reflected in each of the night-blackened windows.

He stepped into the bubble-filled tub and sat down so that he could lounge back against one end and Gracie could sit in front of him and rest against his chest, his legs on either side of her.

"Perfect," he judged.

Gracie sat up straight and glanced at him over her shoulder. "Explain."

He shrugged. "I came in here and used this bathroom after putting the boxes in the attic. You'd left one of the armoire doors open and I saw all these candles on a shelf. I assume your aunt kept them for electrical outages. But I had a better idea." He took her by the shoulders, pulled her back against his chest and said into her hair, "Beautiful, isn't it?"

The candlelight danced with the dark green of the ivy leaves that climbed the walls and the ceiling beams, and gilded everything else. "Beautiful," she agreed, settling into his arms and laying her cheek against his bicep where his arm lined the rim of the tub, thinking that this was a very special man.

He pressed warm lips against the side of her neck. "I love you, Gracie."

He said the words with such sincerity that they made her heart swell into her throat and leave her speechless for a moment. She nuzzled her face into his bicep and kissed him there. "I love you, too," she managed to whisper.

He wrapped her in his arms and they stayed like that, watching the golden light show until the water cooled. Then they dried each other off, blew out the candles and Gabe took her back to the feather bed where he made love to her once more, slowly, tenderly, sweetly, but no less passionately, before they both fell asleep.

Chapter Nine

Gracie spent the next day putting her kitchen in order, seeing to some details that finally settled her into the rest of the house and cooking for the evening's small party. With everything finished just before Dean was scheduled to bring his comic-book dealer over, she took a quick bath and threw on a comfortable pair of jeans and a sleeveless black turtleneck T-shirt.

Her hair was still damp and she hadn't applied any makeup when she answered the doorbell just before five.

"Gracie, this is Brandy Hill. Brandy, my sister," Dean said as they came in.

Gracie took the other woman's outstretched hand and apologized for not being completely put together.

The comic-book dealer was Dean's height exactly, and Gracie couldn't help wondering if the woman always wore perfectly flat shoes with her stirrup pants or if they were just in deference to Dean's small stature.

Brandy was pretty in a plain sort of way, with her long brown hair pulled back into a ponytail and her overlarge tortoiseshell glasses hiding eyes that were a beautiful sable color. And she seemed nice enough, if slightly reserved.

"I asked Brandy to join us for dinner tonight but she has a meeting and can't stay. In fact, she doesn't have a lot of time, so bring out the comics," Dean said the moment the amenities were finished.

Gracie had taken them out of the cedar chest in the attic just after Gabe had left this morning. She brought them into the kitchen from the side table at the foot of the stairs.

"The light in here is the best," she said, setting the comic books in the center of the oak pedestal table.

Brandy put her briefcase on one of the chairs and sat in another. When Dean took the third, Gracie assumed privacy wasn't needed to do the grading and joined them.

Refusing the offer of something to drink, the other woman went right to work. From the briefcase came a small flashlight, a magnifying glass, a pen and a tablet. Then Brandy carefully placed the first issue of Baby Jack Flash directly in front of her as if it might shatter at rougher treatment. Watching, Gracie remembered how she'd handled the magazines herself and was glad this woman hadn't been around to see it.

"I'll go through the whole thing first to make sure there aren't any missing pages," Brandy explained.

But before she did that, she checked the outside. "No spine roll, it's tight, flat and clean. There's perfect luster to both the front and the back covers, and they're centered," she said, though Gracie wasn't sure if Brandy was talking to her and Dean or to herself.

Then Brandy began to slowly, carefully turn the pages. Somehow the faint rustle of each one seemed very loud in the silence. And Brandy proceeded so slowly Gracie felt as if she was watching snow melt. It seemed obvious that the comics were in good condition. Great condition. Was it really necessary to treat each page as if it might crumble at a touch?

"Relax, Gracie," Dean said from the other side of the table as if he knew how fast her heart was beating.

But he didn't have to be taking her pulse, she realized, to know she was tense. She was stiff as a board, her back wasn't even touching the chair.

She took a breath and told herself she was being silly. Of course, this woman would grade the comic books the same as Gabe had.

"The pages are all here and they're white and fresh. This hardly seems to have been looked at," Brandy said next.

Gracie breathed a little easier. Everything would be fine.

But still she studied every move the dealer made as Brandy went on, meticulously searching the comic with the naked eye and magnifying glass, too, commenting as she went along.

There were no tears, no wrinkles, no stains, tape repairs or watermarks. No margin that was too large or small, no color flaked off. There wasn't even a stress line or a wrinkle around a single staple. In fact, there were no imperfections at all, and with each appraisal Gracie relaxed a little more.

"Newsstand quality," Brandy finally judged it.

That wasn't one of the gradings Gracie remembered reading about or hearing Gabe refer to and she felt her heartbeat kick into double time again. "Is newsstand quality better than pristine mint?"

That got Brandy's attention. "Then you do know something about comic book grading?"

"Next to nothing. But I thought pristine mint was the highest."

"It is. And that's what I'm giving this copy. Newsstand quality is just comic-book lingo for a perfect magazine."

Gracie nearly wilted with relief.

Cautiously, Brandy set that magazine aside and went on to the next one. But as the dealer followed the same procedure on both of the others, Gracie stopped worrying.

Of course, the comics would grade out perfectly, just the way Gabe had said. The whole purpose of this exercise was to humor Dean and get him to stop being so suspicious. It wasn't as if there was any reason to believe there would be a discrepancy.

Over an hour had passed by the time Brandy was finally finished with all three comics, judging the other two in pristine-mint condition, as well.

"That's the same grading Gabe gave them," Gracie said, hoping she didn't sound too victorious.

But neither Dean or Brandy seemed to have heard her as the comic-book dealer sat back and smiled at Dean as if she'd just been pleasantly reminded that he was there.

Dean smiled back at her, and as Gracie watched she didn't mind that what she'd said hadn't been acknowledged. Instead, she felt a rush of optimism—for Dean's relationship with this woman, for herself and Gabe, for Gabe and the comics and The Collector's Exchange.

Then Dean seemed to remember what they were doing here and nodded to the magazines. "Her buyer claims to have agreed to sell them to his collectors for sixty thousand dollars."

Brandy's expression sobered with the speed of lightning as she turned to Gracie. "I have a client who I think might pay ninety thousand to get his hands on these. Dean told me you're only interested in selling to your neighbor, but if you accept a penny less than seventy-five you're being robbed."

Goodbye optimism. "Maybe you're overestimating them," Gracie suggested hopefully.

The woman took a small, fat book out of her briefcase, thumbed through it until she reached the page she wanted and handed it to Gracie, pointing a short, well-manicured nail at a particular paragraph. "That's the record of what was paid for the other copies that have turned up in reasonably good condition—twenty thousand each—and they were only rated a near mint or a very fine. That's two and three grades lower than these."

Gracie barely glanced at the page and then gave the book back to Brandy, realizing as she did how cold were her own hands. "I'm sure there's an explanation."

Only polite, sympathetic silence answered her.

Then Brandy closed her briefcase. "Well, I have to get going."

"I'll walk you out to your car," Dean said quickly, as if he was grateful for any diversion.

Gracie went with them as far as the front door, thanking Brandy along the way. Then she returned to the kitchen and put her lasagna in the oven. By the time she'd done that and gotten out the plates, napkins and silverware to set the table, Dean was back.

"Well, what do you think?" he asked her, sounding as if he was sorry his suspicions now seemed founded.

"I told you, there must be an explanation." And that was all she wanted to think. At least at that moment when she was due to have company shortly. "Will you set the table while I go upstairs to put on some mascara and comb my hair?"

"Gracie, I—'

"I really need to finish, Dean. I hate to greet everyone with my hair a mess."

"Okay. Sure," he said.

The phone rang just then, giving Gracie even more of a reason to escape. "I'll answer that upstairs," she said as she headed in that direction.

She made it to her nightstand extension by the fourth ring, leaving her "Hello" a little breathless.

"Gracie? This is Anthony Treble."

Adeline's attorney. "Mr. Treble. Hello," she said, feeling a resurgence of her earlier optimism in a more conservative form. "Thank you for calling. I didn't expect to hear from you on your first day back from vacation. I hope you had a good trip."

He assured her he had, going into a few details of his cruise. Then he said, "So, what can I help you with? Is there a problem with your inheritance from Adeline?"

"Not exactly. It's just that something a little out of the ordinary has come up, and since you're not only my aunt's attorney but have known her as a friend for so many years, I thought you might be able to help."

"Glad to."

Gracie sat down on her bed and told him the whole story from start to finish, including that contacting friends and relatives had proven futile. "So I was hoping that Adeline had spoken to you about the comics and this agreement, because all I need is a confirmation that selling them was what my aunt wanted done, and I'll be more than happy to complete the sale.''

"I'm sorry, Gracie,'' he answered very soberly. "But I don't know anything about an agreement with your aunt to sell anything. And, frankly, I think this is something she would have mentioned to me. We spoke at great length about the request she made in her will that none of what she left to you be sold.''

"Oh,'' was the only thing Gracie could manage to say.

"Of course, you're free to do it, if that's what you feel is right. Part of what Adeline and I discussed was whether or not to make it a stipulation of the will that you absolutely could not sell anything without forfeiting your portion of the inheritance as consequence if you did. But your aunt was sure that wouldn't be necessary. She said that she felt confident that you would honor her wishes if she just let them be known.''

"Yes,'' Gracie said. But that was still all she got in before he went on.

"I don't know how well you're acquainted with this neighbor, but I feel the need to caution you that not everyone is as innocent as they appear. Perhaps you should take into consideration that this person was aware that Adeline was unreachable to substantiate or refute his claim.''

Rather than commenting on that, she said, "Do you happen to know of anyone else she might have confided this to?''

"I'm sorry, but I don't, no.''

"Did she even mention to you that she had sent me a letter just as she was getting ready to leave?''

"We spoke often in that last week as she tied up all the loose ends of her estate and will, but she didn't say anything about writing you. In fact, it seems to me that she would have just included this information in the note she did leave—the one about the neighbor she'd enlisted to show you the workings of the house. That wouldn't be the same neighbor we're discussing now, would it?''

Reluctantly, Gracie confirmed that it was. Then she hurried past the point. "And you're absolutely sure there is no way she can be contacted in Tibet?''

"Absolutely."

"Well," Gracie said, feeling as if a ten-ton weight had just been lowered on her. "Thank you for calling, anyway."

"You know," he went on as if he felt compelled to in spite of the fact that she obviously wanted to end their conversation. "People can be driven to do some very strange things when an inheritance is involved. Sometimes they'll go to great lengths to get their hands on even a bequest to which they have no right whatsoever. I would recommend that you be very cautious. I'd hate to see you do something that would go against Adeline's wishes."

Gabe had just showered and shaved, and was tucking his plum-colored polo shirt into his jeans when he heard his father open the front door and shout, "I'm here."

Poking his head out of his bedroom, Gabe said, "You're early."

"I'm also alone," Eli countered morosely.

That brought Gabe out into the living room. "How come?"

There were dark circles under the older man's eyes. "You never really know a woman until you marry her, Gabe," he said philosophically.

Gabe took a deep breath and let Murf out into the backyard, reminding himself as he did that the speed of his relationship with Gracie left him in no position to criticize. When he came back he said, "What's the problem?"

Eli threw his hands up in the air. "Marge is furious because of this dinner tonight."

"What is there to make her mad? I told Gracie that you said you'd like to see some of Adeline's home movies, so she's having her brother and cousin, you and I and your new wife over for a meal and the movies because she thought we all might get a kick out of it. I thought it was nice of her."

"Of course, it was nice of her. But apparently the whole neighborhood around here has been under the impression all these years that Adeline and I had more than just a friendly relationship. Marge is convinced that Addie and I were lovers. She thinks that's why I want to watch the movies and that I'm rubbing her nose in my affair by even considering that either of us should see them." Eli's frown was dark and deep. "I've discovered that Marge is a very jealous woman."

"Did you explain to her what your relationship with Adeline really was?"

"Over and over again. She didn't believe a word of it. But then, she didn't believe I wasn't flirting with the lady mail carrier yesterday because I said hello to her, or that I wasn't trying to seduce the stewardess on the flight back from Las Vegas. I had to change seats with Marge on the plane so she was between me and the stewardess, and promise that I would never again get the mail until after it was in the box and the carrier was off the property. I tried to think of both of those as flattering, but this time it's just too much. She said she wouldn't even think of going to Gracie's tonight and if I do we're through—the marriage is over."

"Before it began," Gabe said more to himself than to his father.

"Just like my third."

"No, that one lasted a month. This one beats your record."

"Yes, but that wife wasn't anything like I thought she was, either. I had no idea she had a drinking problem."

"And you had no idea my mother was a stickler for clean, or that your second wife only wanted to stay at home all the time, or—"

"I know. I'm a jerk," Eli said sullenly.

"You're not a jerk," Gabe refuted in a hurry, sorry to have made his father feel even worse. "I only meant to point out that you barely knew any of the women you married."

"It's just that they all seem so perfect at first." Eli sat down on the couch, dropping his head into his hands. "Why do I do these things, Gabe?"

That was something Gabe had thought a lot about. "You're a romantic, Pop. Sometimes I think you confuse a simple attraction or infatuation with love. And then you jump into marriage without ever really thinking about what you're doing. Certainly without ever getting to know the women—warts and all."

"Being impulsive has always been my charm," Eli said as if it was an underrated quality whose only failure came in other people's poor response to it. "If Addie had just married me. That would have settled me down."

"Maybe it would have," Gabe agreed. "But only because you really knew her, Pop, her good and bad points. You wouldn't have been marrying someone you'd imagined was perfect only to wake up after the wedding and realize that what you'd thought of the woman was nothing more than a fantasy."

"The fantasies are always so much better than the real thing."

"What are you going to do?" Gabe asked.

The older man frowned up at him as if he was out of his mind. "You can't expect me to live with a woman who's crazy jealous."

"Maybe you should talk to her about it, go into counseling together, try to work through it."

"You know I don't believe in that counseling stuff. Two people are either right together or they're not. And Marge and I are not."

"What do you want to do, then, Pop?"

He shrugged. "Maybe this marriage could be annulled."

Gabe didn't know what to say to that so he opted for practicality. "Did you give up your apartment?"

"No, thank goodness. I still have that. I'll just move back to it." Eli hesitated for a moment, glancing at the wall clock. "And I'm going to Gracie's dinner, too. I want to see those movies. It'll be like touching base with my Addie, and that always made me feel better."

Willy and Dean were sorting through videotapes in the living room when the doorbell rang.

"I'll get it," Gracie called to them from the kitchen.

Gabe and his father were on the porch when she opened the door. The older man looked somewhat down in the mouth, and Gabe appeared pretty somber himself.

Maybe everybody had had a bad day.

Gracie let them in and once the amenities had been exchanged, Eli said, "Marge won't be joining us, Gracie. I'm sorry."

"She's not sick, I hope."

The older man shook his head. "No, she's well. She's just not your aunt," he said enigmatically. Then he greeted Dean and Willy and turned into the living room.

"Huh?" Gracie said to Gabe in a voice soft enough for his ears only.

"Let's go check on whatever it is you have in the oven," he answered, taking her elbow and steering her to the kitchen.

The first thing he did when they got there was to pull her into a kiss. Then, with his arms slung around her waist, he explained his father's most recent marital problems. At the end of it he shrugged his shoulders. "So, another one bites the dust," he said, his tone making it clear that he took his father's pattern more seriously than the glib comment might make it sound.

"I'm sorry," Gracie said, because she could see how this disturbed him.

"Me, too. More sorry than my father is, it seems."

Just then the sound of Eli's laughter carried to them.

Gabe glanced in the direction of the living room and then down at Gracie. "He isn't going to let a little thing like the end of his marriage ruin his evening, so I don't think we should."

"Well, dinner's ready. We could go ahead and eat."

"In a minute," he said, pulling her close and resting his chin on her head.

His body around hers was big and warm and it felt good to Gracie. Comfortable. Soothing. A haven. And yet, what if the haven she needed was *from* him?

Still, she couldn't move out of his arms for a moment longer, giving in to the need to be close to him, to block out everything else.

"Oh, this feels good," he said into her hair.

Maybe too good. What if he really was just making up the story about Adeline agreeing to sell him the comics? What kind of a person did that make him?

Gracie straightened away from him and went to the refrigerator as if it were home base. "You can take the salad into the dining room and call everyone to the table."

If Eli had regrets or bad feelings about his brief seventh marriage he didn't show them. Instead, he kept the dinner conversation alive, peppering it with jokes that made everyone laugh.

It amazed Gracie that he could be so cavalier about what had happened with his latest relationship, but she was grateful not to be required for much more than passing plates and filling wineglasses. She had too much on her mind to be a more active hostess.

All through dinner she couldn't help watching Gabe. Lord, but he was an attractive man. And he had such a potent effect on her.

Was she just very needy and vulnerable because it was so soon after Burt's death? Was she so needy and vulnerable that she was overlooking the kind of character flaw that would allow him to lie about the comics and Adeline? Dean thought so. Adeline's lawyer suspected Gabe. Most of her aunt's friends and relatives had voiced doubts about his story. Even Willy was wavering slightly, taking more seriously Dean's claim that Gabe was not on the up-and-up.

And yet.

Could Gabe make her feel so good if beneath it all he was the kind of man who could lie and lay claim to something he had no right to? Would being with him seem so perfect if their relationship was based on dishonesty and deceit?

It didn't seem so.

But it was possible she was being naive. That she was being too trusting, just the way Dean said she was. It was possible that so soon after Burt's death her own instincts were off kilter. It was possible that her attraction to Gabe was blinding her.

And she had to face those possibilities.

"What a delicious meal!" Eli said, breaking into her thoughts.

One glance around told Gracie that she was the only one who hadn't cleaned the plate and pushed it away. She urged everyone to have more and when no one did, she took her napkin from her lap to set on the table and suggested they leave everything and have coffee in the living room while they started the movies.

"Are you okay?" Gabe asked as he helped her with the coffee in the kitchen. "You hardly touched your food."

"I'm fine," she assured him, a little too brightly. "I guess I must have done too much sampling before we sat down to eat. I wasn't very hungry."

He smiled a little crookedly. "Then can I assume that you were daydreaming instead of eating and that's why every time I looked up you were staring at me as if you were in a trance?"

"Who, me? Staring? In a trance? You must be imagining things." She made light of it.

"I was imagining things, all right. I've heard all my father's jokes and stories a hundred times. I had something much more interesting on my mind," he said, wriggling his eyebrows up and down lasciviously. "I can't wait to get you in the dark."

"Careful," she advised. "My brother has a protective streak where I'm concerned."

"I already figured that out. I caught him giving me a warning glare every so often through dinner. Shall I tell him that my intentions are honorable?"

Are-they? she was tempted to ask. But instead, she said, "No, I don't think that would be a good idea." Then she picked up the tray full of cups, spoons, sugar and cream, and nodded toward the coffeepot. "Why don't you take that in for me? I don't think it would be a good idea for us to have too long a rendezvous in here, either."

"Ah, I see. Your brother really is a spoilsport," Gabe joked as he followed her into the living room.

Willy and Dean were on the couch, Eli had taken the chair and that left Gabe and Gracie the floor in front of the coffee table.

Gabe sat there while Gracie turned on the TV and put the cassette in. "I had all the old reels transferred to videotape because the projector was broken and this is so much easier," she explained as she did. "Plus, they could compile everything on just a few tapes."

Then, with a remote control in hand, she joined Gabe. It was purely by accident that when she did, sitting side by side with their backs against the coffee table, Gabe's leg ran the length of hers, their thighs touching.

Gracie wondered if she should move to stop the warm, tingling sensation that any contact with him elicited. But in the end she stayed where she was, giving in to the innocent sensual pleasure.

Willy turned off the lights. "It's showtime," she called, and Gracie started the movie.

The beginning of the video showed scenes of Gracie, Dean and Willy as kids. There were shots of them building a clubhouse out of a big box, of them dressed in Halloween costumes, and of them wrestling in the snow with Adeline, the four of them moving in and out of the range of the camera lens left stationary.

This portion of the tape traced the three cousins through their teenage years, through high school graduations and on into adulthood where there was shot after shot of holiday dinners.

Gracie's wedding to Burt came next and she was relieved to watch it with a minimum of pain. It helped immensely to have Gabe's hand on her knee, squeezing just enough to let her know he understood that this couldn't be easy for her.

Then there was a snowy lapse and shots began of Eli with the tall, skinny Adeline towering above him by a good four inches. They were young, Eli's hair was as dark as Gabe's and Adeline's was coal black, tied up in her ever-present short ponytail at the crown of her head.

Along with films taken around town or on special occasions like birthdays or holidays, or at events like Eli's retirement, there were some of every trip they'd ever taken together—something they did often between Eli's many marriages.

Time could be clocked by the graying of their hair, the wrinkling of their faces, the changes in their clothing styles as they stood at the Grand Canyon, ate tacos in front of a New Mexico sign, or stared in awe at the lights of the strip in Las Vegas. In every shot they were arm in arm, or mugging for the stand-held camera.

Black-and-white static showed a lapse again and then what began were more recent films. In some of them both Gabe and Eli appeared, and in one Adeline stood between them, a hand on each of their shoulders while she did a cancan dance, her now completely white ponytail bobbing around gaily.

The latest movies took on a feeling of proud parents filming their son as Eli and Adeline became less active and did more clowning around on the sidelines and Gabe became the focus of the films.

He shoveled snow from Adeline's walks as she pretended to crack a whip behind him and Eli mimed a bent and decrepit old man who couldn't lift so much as a snowball. Or Gabe mowed Adeline's grass while she and Eli went down on all fours, pretending to chew their cud like two cows out to pasture.

There were two shots of Gabe alone—up in the tree in the front yard, acting like a monkey before cutting a branch, and pushing Adeline's car out of a snowdrift at the foot of the driveway. And there was one of Gabe carrying Adeline across the threshold while Eli held the door open. Adeline's foot was in a cast from a fall the summer before, and she was pinching Gabe's cheek as if to say what a good boy he was.

In the last scenes Gabe and Adeline sat alone on the front steps laughing and making faces for the camera like two consummate hams, looking as if they were having a wonderful time.

"I didn't realize what good friends you and my aunt really were," Gracie said when the movies ended and everyone stood, stretched and started to clear away the coffee things.

"They were bosom buddies," Willy supplied before Gabe could answer.

"I liked her. She was fun," he put in as he followed Willy and his father out of the living room.

"She also owned something he wanted," Dean whispered to Gracie when everyone else was out of earshot.

In the kitchen both Eli and Willy exclaimed over how late it had gotten and when Gracie assured them she didn't want help with the dishes, they said good-night.

Once they were gone, Dean yawned. "I'm too tired to drive home. How about if I sleep here tonight, Gracie?"

Gracie saw the ploy for what it was. Her brother wanted to make sure she wasn't left alone with Gabe. And for the first time since she'd met him, Gracie wasn't altogether sure she wanted to be left alone with him. She had a lot of thinking to do and being near Gabe was counterproductive to that.

"I don't mind if you stay," she assured Dean.

"Well," Gabe put in, not quite hiding his disappointment at not being the last to leave, "I guess I'd better head home, too."

As she'd done with Eli and Willy, Gracie walked him to the door. But this time Dean came, too.

"Good night, Dean," Gabe said, obviously hoping that would get rid of him. But Dean said good-night and stayed anyway.

Gabe opted for ignoring him. With one hand on Gracie's waist he brought her nearer. "I'll talk to you tomorrow," he said in a low, intimate voice just before he kissed her, softly, slowly, as if it would build into something more if only they didn't have an audience.

But they did have one and Gracie was all too aware of it. She ended the kiss with a hand on his chest. "Tomorrow," she said then, not intending the word to come out sounding like a promise.

Gabe smiled, that intimate, rebel grin of his, and kissed her once more briefly before he left.

"Do you want to talk about…anything?" Dean asked as they turned off the lights and locked up.

"No, I'm pretty beat, too. I'd just like to go to bed," she told him, knowing he wanted to discuss Gabe and the comics.

Her brother didn't push it. Instead, they went upstairs, Gracie to the master bedroom and Dean to the guest room.

But once her door was closed she turned to face the bed she and Gabe had shared the night before.

Was the man who had made love to her there capable of lying about an agreement with her aunt in order to gain the comics?

Everyone else seemed to think so.

And Gracie wished she didn't.

But she kept remembering the care with which he'd straightened the sports cards in the display case at The Collector's Exchange. She could hear the affection in his references to the shop, to its contents, the excitement in his voice when he'd talked to those boys. In her mind's eye she could see the joy in his face as he'd opened those boxes of comic books he was handling for the other dealer and discovered some he hadn't seen before.

The Collector's Exchange meant a great deal to Gabe.

So much, she was afraid, that he'd do just about anything to keep it going.

Chapter Ten

The sound of Dean doing dishes downstairs woke Gracie early the next morning. Sleep had allowed her to escape thinking about the situation with Gabe and the comics, but there was something agitated in the clatter coming from the kitchen that reminded her. Or maybe the noise was no more than normal and the uneasiness was her own, making her perceive the sounds as overly loud. But either way she woke with the sure knowledge that she had to face the issue of the comic books today. Beginning with Dean.

"The broom is in the laundry room," she said as she came into the kitchen seconds after a plate hit the floor.

"Sorry," Dean muttered as he went into the small connecting room.

Gracie took over loading the dishwasher while he swept up the broken china.

"Sleep well?" she asked.

"Hardly at all." Dean emptied the dustpan into the trash, replaced the broom and came back, standing beside her at the sink.

Wearing his clothes from the night before, his hair combed, he would have looked as if no time at all had passed if not for the slight shadow of his beard. "I was up most of the night thinking and I can't keep my mouth shut anymore. I have to talk about this, Gracie," he said as if Brandy Hill had just walked out the door.

"Okay."

"Look, I don't care about those comics—selling them or not makes no difference to me. Frankly, I think Adeline's request that you not sell anything was as nutty as Adeline, and I'd like to see you make the money. Willy and I both would. It doesn't seem fair that she and I inherited all the capital assets. Especially when you consider how old this house is and how many repairs it's going to need. We hate to see you use Burt's insurance money on that."

Gracie opened her mouth to say that money was not a problem but before the words could come out, Dean went on.

"You can even sell the comics to Duran if you want, though it would irk me to know this con job succeeded for him and I'd hate to see you cheated." Dean put his hand on her shoulders, turning her only slightly to look into her face with earnest, concerned eyes the same green color as Gracie's. "But what really worries me is your personal relationship with someone who would do all he has done."

"*All?*"

Dean raised a finger for every point he made. "First he comes here claiming that he had an arrangement to get his hands on something of Adeline's that she probably refused to let go of the same way she refused to sell anything else around here. Second, he puts pressure on you by claiming there's a lawsuit against him. Third, you find out that the price he swears Adeline agreed to is fifteen to thirty thousand dollars less than what the comics are worth. Fourth—"

But that fourth finger just stuck out there in the air without a reason.

"Fourth?" Gracie prompted out of curiosity.

Dean hesitated a moment before he forged on as if he were blurting out the painful truth. "I realize this is unflattering and I don't want you to take it personally because I think it has to do with him, not with you. But you can't know for sure that he isn't seducing you just to get hold of what he wants. It's possible that the minute you hand over the comics you'll never see or hear from him again. He wouldn't be the first man to figure a single woman was easy prey and to romance her into getting himself what he wanted."

Gracie closed the dishwasher.

"You can't go on defending him," Dean said before she even had, sounding frustrated and almost frantic to open her eyes to what he obviously believed he saw so clearly. "Nobody—not a relative, not a friend, not the attorney, not even Eli—was aware of any arrangement to sell the comics. And not one of them—people who were her longtime friends and most likely knew her better than we did—believe that Adeline would do it."

Gracie washed off the countertop and defended Gabe anyway. "What we do know about our aunt is that if anyone told her something in confidence, not even torture would get it out of her—remember all those speeding tickets you went to her with the first year you got your driver's license? She helped you take care of them without ever telling a soul. It seems possible that this situation falls into that category."

"What about the letter, then?" he demanded. "Adeline made sure you got the note about Duran showing you the ropes of the house. Why would she have trusted a more important letter to a postal system that she knew was unreliable? Why didn't she leave that with her lawyer, too, to make sure you got it?"

Gracie couldn't argue with a good point. Especially when it was something she'd wondered about herself. But she didn't have to, as Dean went on.

"What more does it take to convince you that there's something shady about the whole situation with this guy?"

"I haven't found confirmation for his claim, but I also haven't found any evidence that he's not telling the truth, either."

Her brother threw his hands up in the air. "You're too trusting, Gracie."

"I have to give him the benefit of the doubt. He deserves the chance to at least defend himself."

"And if he can't? Or if his defense is as weak as the rest of his story?"

"Then I don't know what I'll do," she admitted, some of her own frustration bursting out. She took a breath and looked at the clock on the stove. "Shouldn't you be getting home?" she said, thinking that she had enough to deal with at the moment without having Dean's protectiveness to handle on top of it.

But he didn't take the hint. "Are you going to confront him?"

"Just as soon as you get out of here. I thought I'd go over to his house."

"I think I should stay here just in case you need me."

"I think you've been watching too many detective shows and reading too many mysteries. You can't truly think I'm in any kind of danger."

"I truly think that anything is possible." He leaned against the counter as if he'd taken root. "And I'm staying right here until you get back."

"Dean—"

"Be glad I'm not insisting on going with you or having him come here so I can be right at your elbow if you need me."

Gracie gave up. She wasn't as unconcerned with this whole situation as she'd shown her brother. Not even close. And she had too much on her mind to go on with this discussion.

"Suit yourself. Stay if you want," she finally told Dean. "As soon as I throw on my sweat suit and comb my hair, I'm going across the street."

She handed him the dishrag and marched upstairs, maintaining the image of Gabe's staunchest advocate. But in truth it was difficult for her to feel sure it was warranted anymore.

Still, there was one question yet to be asked. Why was there such a difference in what Gabe wanted to pay for the Baby Jack Flash comics and what they were worth?

"Please have a good answer," she whispered as she slipped out of her bathrobe and reached for her sweat suit.

Gabe's front door was open when Gracie walked up to it, but rather than calling through the screen she rang the doorbell. Somehow this errand made her feel a formality she didn't usually have with him.

"Is that you, Pop?" Gabe's voice sounded as if it came from down the hall.

"No, it's me," Gracie called back.

There was a momentary silence before Gabe appeared, dressed in his morning-walk attire—those old cutoff jeans with the pockets peeking out from underneath the ragged fringe of many washings, and the faded red tank top that left part of his chest and all of his muscular arms visible.

He pushed the screen open but blocked the doorway with his big body. With one hand on the upper part of the jamb he leaned against the side of it. "I was hoping you'd sneak out when your brother went to sleep last night. You're a little late," he teased, aiming that rebel grin down at her.

Gracie's pulse picked up speed and she tried to ignore how dangerously good he looked even in ratty clothes. "We need to talk," she said.

His grin disappeared and his busy eyebrows pulled together. "Modern man has learned to hate that phrase." He stepped out of the way. "Come in."

Murf was sleeping in the middle of the couch in the living room. His eyelids looked heavy as he lifted them only to half-mast to acknowledge Gracie's entrance and then closed them again. Feeling very nervous, Gracie hid it by saying hello to the dog, petting his velvety head.

"What's up?" Gabe asked.

She knew she couldn't do this with her back to him, so she took a deep breath and turned to face him, finding him standing with his weight on one hip, his arms crossed over his stomach, covering the hole in his shirt that let her catch glimpses of his hard belly. She had the unholy urge to go to him, to have those arms open for her and then fold around her. But, of course, that was the last thing she could do.

"We have to talk about the comics," she said grimly.

Gabe's expression darkened. His brows pulled together even more. "I take it you're not over here to announce that we can go through with the sale this afternoon?"

She shook her head. "I've spoken to Adeline's attorney."

"And he doesn't know anything about my agreement with your aunt."

Was that a guess or a statement of a fact he knew already because there was no agreement to know about?

Gracie fought the ugly thought. "No, Adeline didn't tell him anything about selling the comics or writing to me just before she left...or anything. Except how strongly she felt about her things not being sold." Gracie added that last part a little more softly than the rest.

"Damn."

"There's more." But she couldn't meet his eyes. She went back to petting Murf's cocoa-colored head, staring at the dog instead. "I told you Dean is very protective of me," she began.

"I saw that for myself last night."

"Well, he thought that it was best to get some information on the comics themselves and this sort of a transaction, since I'm completely in the dark about it." Again she finished in a softer, more hesitant voice. "He contacted another dealer through a friend of his."

When Gabe didn't say anything for a moment she glanced at him, finding that his expression had hardened slightly. "Are you taking rival bids?" he asked very formally, sounding like an angry, but still very professional, businessman.

"No, no, it's nothing like that. I made it clear that I'll sell the comics to you or no one at all. It's like I said, he just thought I should be informed. Anyway, the woman's name is Brandy Hill."

"I've met her a couple of times at conventions."

"She came by yesterday to take a look at the comics. She agreed with your grading, giving all three a pristine-mint rating. But when we told her about the price you and Adeline had agreed on she was pretty surprised. She said that they're worth a lot more than that."

"She's right." His tone was tight and clipped.

And Gracie was so relieved to hear that Gabe agreed that she almost relaxed. "I told Dean that there was an explanation for the difference."

She waited to hear it. But Gabe seemed lost in thought and wasn't forthcoming. She couldn't help wondering if he was trying to think of a plausible story. Wouldn't the truth come easily, after all?

Then he broke into her thoughts with a less than patient tone of voice. "I was under the impression that you were asking around for confirmation of your aunt's intentions so you could sell the comics in good conscience, not because you thought I was trying to pull a fast one on you."

She forced herself to face him then, with a straight back and a level gaze. "I was only looking for confirmation, but Dean—" She stopped short, at a loss for how to word this. To say her brother had been suspicious was so insulting. Even to say that Dean thought she was too trusting didn't sound good. She settled on, "Dean was just trying to help. He's a worrier. But he's not the only person who was uneasy with this. Even Adeline's lawyer advised caution, and there were a lot of the friends and relatives who were surprised that she had agreed to sell anything—your father included." Gracie stopped abruptly. She'd said too much and she knew it.

Gabe breathed an ironic laugh. "Let me see if I understand this. There's a whole contingent that suspects I'm lying?"

"It's just been hard for a lot of people to think of my aunt selling something. You knew her, surely you know that it was almost impossible for her to put a price tag on anything."

His eyes captured hers and held them. "What about you, Gracie? What have you been thinking?"

"That any minute someone was going to tell me Adeline had told them about the deal," she answered without hesitation because it was true. At least, it had been until yesterday. "But I would like to understand why the selling price is so low."

Again he stared at her without speaking, as if wondering if he could belive that she had trusted him, and Gracie felt pinned to the wall by the piercing gaze of those eyes that were more smoky than blue now. But she didn't waver. She had the right to an answer.

Finally he gave it. "Adeline set the price. I told her I could get more for the comics, but she wouldn't listen to me."

"Why not?"

"The sole reason for her deciding to sell was to help The Collector's Exchange get on its feet. I'd confided to her how important it was to connect with the group that was referred to me, and offering the Baby Jack Flash issues was the bait to lure them in. Once we knew they were interested I explained to her the prices of past sales and told her what I thought these buyers would pay. But she insisted on going lower to sweeten the deal, to make absolutely sure they were impressed enough to stick with me from here on."

"But wouldn't it have been impressive enough just to have unearthed rare issues and be the dealer who was handling the sale of them?"

"Yes, and I told her that. But in case you aren't aware of it, your aunt is a very stubborn, headstrong woman. She was determined to make this look like a great coup I alone had accomplished. She said she didn't care about the money and she knew you wouldn't, either, so the group got a bargain price. It was worth it to her to give The Collector's Exchange a boost. She said to consider it an investment in my business." He sighed. "So what's it going to be? Are you here to tell me you definitely won't sell?"

Without something concrete to prove this exception to her aunt's wishes, it seemed to Gracie that that was just what she should tell him. Without confirmation, wasn't selling the comics a betrayal of Adeline's trust in her—the whole reason Adeline had left her what she had?

But Gracie couldn't make herself tell Gabe the deal was off. And that made her worry that she was thinking with her emotions. Emotions that had ricocheted from love and contentment with Burt to devastating grief over his death, to love for Gabe. All in the span of six short months. Emotions that could well be leaving her instincts and her judgment out of whack.

"I can't give you an answer right now," she said. "I'm going to need to think about it."

Gabe's expression was blank. He didn't move as she went to the door. He didn't even look at her, and that gave Gracie a moment of doubt. Was it possible that Dean was right? That what had been between them personally was trumped up on Gabe's part to make her more inclined to sell him the comics?

But just as her hand touched the screen to push it open he was at her side, grasping her arm to stop her.

Gracie looked up at his face. His expression was filled with as much turmoil as she was feeling at that moment. Turmoil that wouldn't be there if his heart wasn't involved, too.

He pursed his lips together in a strained smile and squeezed her arm. "I'm sorry to put you through this," he said in a deep, gravelly voice.

"I'm sorry, too," she answered so softly it was barely audible.

He dropped his forehead to her hair in a way that said they were in this together. "You'll let me know as soon as you decide?"

"You'll be the first," she said in a feeble attempt to lessen some of the tension that wrapped them like a straitjacket.

He raised his head from hers and looked directly into her eyes again for a moment more, tracing soothing circles on her arm with his thumb.

Then he opened the screen for her and Gracie left beneath the tunnel of his big body.

Chapter Eleven

Eli arrived for their morning walk not five minutes after Gracie left Gabe's house. The older man kept up a running conversation as they exercised, without seeming to notice that his son had very little to say in response to his complaints about the difficulties of convincing his new wife to have their marriage annulled. But Gabe couldn't concentrate while his thoughts were on all that Gracie had said.

Had she been suspicious of him all this time?

That was hard to believe. How could they have gotten so close if that were the case?

They couldn't have, he decided. Gracie was no fool. If she thought he was lying to her about the agreement with her aunt there was no way she would have had anything to do with him.

No, the suspicions weren't hers. At least, not all along. Not even as late as the day before—hadn't she said that she'd told her brother that there was an explanation for the low selling price on the comics, defending him to Dean?

But there had been suspicion in this morning's question. Gabe had seen it. Sensed it. Suspicion of her own.

Still, she'd clearly been holding out hope that he could put her mind to rest. He'd seen that in her, too. She'd given him the benefit of the doubt in spite of what Gabe had to admit was a pretty questionable situation—a stranger's unverifiable claim to a fortune in comic books.

"Are you listening to anything I've said?" Eli's impatient voice interrupted his thoughts as they hit the halfway point.

Gabe remembered snatches of his father's conversation. He tried to recall the most recent—something about having lunch with the attorney who had handled all of the dissolutions of Eli's marriages.

"You're seeing your lawyer today?" Gabe guessed.

"Yes. Do you want to join us? Maybe get his opinion on that lawsuit against you?"

"I don't think a divorce lawyer's opinion would make much difference. But thanks, anyway."

Eli finished their walk with more marital laments, but once they reached home he was in a hurry, so he said goodbye and headed for his car.

Gabe went inside and as he did his father's earlier mention of the lawsuit brought another thought to mind. If Gracie didn't sell him the comics, not only would that cause the suit against him to go to court, but Simonesque could call her as a witness against him.

"Great," he said out loud as he got into the shower.

She'd have to testify if she was called. She'd have to say that she hadn't sold the comics because she didn't believe he actually had an agreement with her aunt. There wouldn't be any way out of it, or anything else she could say. And it would back up the group's claim that he had misled them to get them to sell their other issues and earn himself a commission on the sale.

Gabe stopped soaping his chest in midswirl. And what would happen to their relationship if she didn't sell him the comics and all of this came to pass? Would he resent it and the havoc it wreaked on his life? Would his feelings for her change?

He imagined the worst of the possible outcomes of not being able to get hold of the comics: losing The Collector's Exchange because he needed the commission to keep him afloat financially; having to go back into the corporate rat race; losing the lawsuit and being forced to pay exorbitant damages, not to mention legal fees, maybe losing his house to pay those fees....

The prospect was bleak.

And yet, worse than all of that was the thought of facing it without Gracie. Of losing her.

Gabe closed his eyes and stood directly under the spray of the shower, letting it rain down over his face.

He couldn't lose her. He loved her. And with or without the comic books he wanted her in his life. Permanently.

His heart was beating hard and he stepped out from under the water to take a breath.

Was he actually thinking about marriage?

Surprised with himself, he realized he was. He was ready to jump into marriage with a woman he'd only recently met. Just like his father.

But even the thought of his father's rocky marital history didn't dampen his desire to make Gracie his wife. Was this what his father had referred to before? Feelings having a will of their own, overriding good judgment?

But no matter how Gabe looked at it, he couldn't see his relationship with Gracie as anything like those his father had had with seven wives.

Yes, Gabe's relationship with Gracie had happened fast. But he hadn't lost his head. He was thinking clearly enough to know that in spite of all the destruction Gracie could cause in his life with one simple *no,* he still wanted her to marry him.

And that, he knew without a doubt, was real love.

But the question was, if she didn't believe he was telling the truth about the comics, would she want anything at all to do with him?

Dean was on the telephone with Brandy when Gracie crossed the street from Gabe's house. While he ended his phone call she did a load of laundry so as not to eavesdrop. She was just closing the lid on the washing machine when he appeared at the mud-room door.

"Well, what did your neighbor have to say for himself?"

Gracie relayed Gabe's explanation for the price discrepancy on the comics.

"I don't believe it," Dean said flatly when she was finished.

"I didn't think you would."

"Do you?"

Gracie didn't answer that directly as she went past her brother back into the kitchen. "I'll tell you what I'm going to do. I'm heading up to the attic to bring down that old horse tricycle, take it out to the garage where I can sand and scrape it to my heart's content, and think in peace. In other words, I'm going to work and so should you. And there's not anything else I can tell you right now because that's all I know for sure," she said, ending more impatiently than she'd begun as her own frustration level rose.

"I've only been trying to help," he pointed out.

"I know that, Dean. But you've done all you can and now it's just a matter of me having to make up my own mind."

He held up his hand in surrender. "Okay. I'm going."

"Thank you."

"But first you better let me help you get that tricycle down from the attic. It's not small."

"That you can do," she agreed.

Between the two of them, getting the antique bike downstairs and outside wasn't too much of an ordeal. And then, good to his word, Dean left her alone in the garage.

"It's just you and me, kid," she told the horse, smoothing its carved mane as if it were real. Then she went to the tool chest against the back wall of the garage, opening the bottom drawer to take out three sheets of sandpaper.

As she turned to the tricycle again her gaze caught on the reflection of the sun and sky in the bathroom windows across the yard. It shimmered there as if on water and for a moment she had the most intense flashback to the cruise she and Burt had taken for their fifteenth anniversary. They had shared breakfast each of the five mornings on the ship's deck, looking out at the ocean mirroring clear blue skies and bright lemon suns.

The memory was so vivid it could have been yesterday. But really, very little time had passed since then, she realized, not even a year. Barely ten months.

And suddenly more events came to mind. Burt had still been alive for her birthday just nine months ago. He'd been alive at Christmas and at New Year's. He'd been alive for his own birthday on the thirteenth of January of this very same year. And here it was, only the middle of summer. . . .

Somehow putting the passage of time in terms of events made it seem much less than thinking about the months, and it left Gracie feeling very off balance.

"Work," she ordered herself out loud to regain her equilibrium. Burt and the passage of time weren't what she came out here to think about, after all.

She wrapped the sandpaper around her hand and started on the horse's saddle, ridding it of several layers of paint that had repaired the wear and tear of many riders.

So, she thought, did she believe Gabe's claim that Adeline had intended to sell the comics?

It was hard for her not to, she admitted.

Did that mean she was just being too trusting, the way Dean thought she was?

"Well, I come by it naturally," she defended herself, as if her brother was there accusing her. "Being too trusting is just something else I inherited from Adeline."

That rang a bell in her mind.

Adeline was a very trusting person. But more specifically, she had trusted Gabe. Her aunt had given him a key to her house. The house where the comics were.

Now *that* was trust.

But Adeline had been very fond of Gabe. It was more than obvious in the home movies in which he'd starred. And Gabe had clearly been fond of Adeline. After all, the movies proved how much he'd helped her with the heavier chores of home owning—the snow shoveling, lawn mowing, branch cutting. He'd even carried her into the house when she broke her leg, which was above and beyond the call of a good neighbor.

But then Gabe and Adeline would have been more than friendly neighbors no matter what, Gracie thought, remembering the tone of the films that had reminded her of parents taking pictures of a child they shared. Gabe was Eli's son. The son of Adeline's dearest friend—a man she had loved—would have had a special place in Adeline's heart regardless of where he lived or what he'd done. It would only have been frosting on the cake for Adeline to have found him helpful and kind and fun to be with, too.

"Maybe we've been looking at this from the wrong perspective," Gracie told the horse.

Everyone, including Gracie, had been trying to picture Adeline selling something she'd kept for years, and that was too unlike her aunt to be believable. But what no one had taken into consideration was that it was definitely Adeline's nature to want to help someone she cared about. And Gracie didn't doubt for a minute that her aunt had cared about Gabe.

It occurred to her, then, that Adeline wanting to help Gabe was a common thread that wound through everything. Wanting to help Gabe stay in business. To help the group of collectors to be impressed with him. To cause them to believe Gabe had made a great coup and pulled off getting them a bargain at the same time.

Actually, in a way, selling the comics for less than they were worth might even have taken away that aspect Adeline had always hated of reducing her special belongings to cash value. Taking money for something she owned could well have been just a necessary evil to accomplish all she wanted for Gabe.

Gracie stopped sanding and looked up at Gabe's house. "Of course," she said as if the truth had been there for her to see all along.

* * *

Gracie was watching for Gabe when he got home that evening. She headed across the street as he pulled into the garage and he must have seen her in his rearview mirror because he opened his front door to her before she could even knock.

"Hi," he said. Holding the screen for her, his smile welcomed her in spite of the question in his tone.

She went in, going to the center of the living room before she turned to him. "I know you're probably tired of dealing with comic books after doing it all day, but I wondered if maybe you had the stamina for just a little more."

His smile evolved into one that was intimate as he stayed near the door much as he had this morning when she'd come to tell him bad news. Only this time he wore khaki slacks and a plaid shirt that brought out the blue in his eyes. "I have plenty of stamina for anything you have in mind," he answered and Gracie couldn't be sure whether his eyes dropped to her breasts or to the cedar box she held there like a schoolgirl carrying books.

"What's up?" he asked.

"Today I started to sand an old tricycle I found in the attic. I always think better when I'm working."

He crossed his arms over his broad chest and slung his weight on one hip. "Okay," he said, as if this tidbit of information should mean something to him.

"When I was a kid Dean and Willy used to play tricks on me—one of the pitfalls of being the youngest," she went on. "They called it Amazing Gracie. They'd make up some outrageous story—signs of UFOs in the empty lot, things like that—and they'd come to me and do a convincing recounting of it. I was pretty gullible and for a long time I fell for every one. They got a big kick out of fooling me, watching my eyes get big and my mouth drop open in amazement. Then they'd laugh their heads off because I was dumb enough to believe them."

"Want me to beat them up for you?" he offered sympathetically, but still looking and sounding confused.

"No, I caught on after a while. I even got them back once or twice. But the point is, I've always been a trusting person—*too* trusting, Dean says. And that's part of what he's been worried about over the comics. Today, when I was working, I wondered if that was true, and in a roundabout way I started to think about my aunt and her nature, and her relationship with you. And I realized what should have occurred to me a lot earlier than this."

"Which is?"

"That while it was unlike Adeline to sell any of her belongings, it was very much like her to want to help out someone she cared about. You."

Gabe just watched her.

"Anyway, I realized that I had confirmation of her intentions to let you sell the comics in things like the house key she'd trusted you with, and seeing you in those home movies of hers, and the fact that you're Eli's son." She held out the cedar box. "So, here. Handle the sale. I hope it isn't too late."

But he didn't immediately take her offering. "You're sure?"

"Positive."

"And your brother?"

"I called and told him this a little while ago. He still thinks I'm too trusting."

"But that's all right with you?"

"I don't have any doubts about this, if that's what you mean. So I don't have to have Dean's approval."

Gabe accepted the box with one hand and reached for Gracie with the other, pulling her up close against him and holding her there. "I'm going to have to find a good way of thanking you for this," he said in a barrel-deep voice.

"I didn't do anything but gum up the works. It's Adeline who deserves the thanks."

"Play proxy," he suggested, kissing her.

His lips were warm and soft on hers and Gracie melted beneath them, pleased that this had worked out for the best.

"I came to some realizations of my own today," he said then. Keeping his arm around her, he brought her with him to set the comics on the coffee table and sit on the couch.

"Did you realize something profound?" she teased him.

"Mmm. That even if you decided not to let me sell the comics I still wanted you in my life. That I love you and nothing can shake it. I realized that I wanted you to marry me."

"Marry you." Everything went very still inside her.

He smiled. "Is that the look that Amazing Gracie elicited? Wide-eyed, openmouthed shock?"

She tried to smile but her cheeks quivered and wouldn't let her lips hang on to it. "You must have really wanted those comics to consider marrying me to get them." She tried to make a joke out of it.

"You weren't listening—I said that even if you'd decided you couldn't sell them I still wanted you to marry me."

Gracie's thoughts suddenly did a fast flip backward through the same timetable she'd thought of this morning and her sense of balance tipped again.

"Gabe—"

He must have felt her stiffen away from him because he took his arm from around her and leaned slightly forward to look into her face. "I know what you're going to say—it's too soon. I thought about the same thing. Ever since I met you I've been worried about how fast this relationship has developed. Believe me, with my father's track record for this same thing, it's been on my mind. I swore it would never happen to me."

He took her hands between both of his. "But Gracie, it has happened and the speed of it doesn't matter. I'm in love with you. So much in love with you that if you'd walked in here tonight and said you absolutely were not going to let those comics go, I'd still be asking you to marry me. That's not at all like the image of perfection that blinds my father every time he jumps into another marriage. This came out of imagining the worst."

Gracie could only shake her head as she tried to tamp down on a feeling of panic. "It's too soon for me," she blurted out. "Everything has happened too fast. I've known it all along but I've been ignoring my own little red flags. We barely know each other."

"I thought the same thing," he said patiently. "That's what I lecture my father on, that he marries these women before he knows them. But I do know you, Gracie. I know you're a warm, kind, considerate, intelligent, caring woman. I know you have a level head on your shoulders. I know you aren't easily swayed by what other people think, that you make your own decisions. That—"

"I just can't." She cut him off.

"I also know," he went on anyway, in a soft, compassionate voice, "that not long ago you lost the husband you loved dearly. But I'm not worried that you haven't worked through that or that I can't help you work through whatever is left to deal with. I honestly don't believe that I'm just a replacement—like a spare part. I think what we've found together is right. It's perfect. And I think you know it, too. I think that our relationship has happened so fast and even so soon after your husband's death *because* it's right and perfect. That it's happened in spite of everything else.''

Her hands were shaking and she pulled them out of his grip to clamp them in her lap and stop it. "Or maybe we just got carried away. Maybe we went a little crazy. Maybe this just happens to all recent widows. I don't know. But I can't do this.''

She stood up in a hurry and went to the door, desperate to regain some balance.

Gabe caught her just as she was about to open it, turning her around to face him. "I shouldn't have hit you with a marriage proposal out of the blue. I didn't mean to scare you. Let's talk about it.''

"This whole relationship is out of the blue. I don't need to talk about it. I shouldn't have even gotten involved with someone this soon, let alone consider getting married.''

"Think about it, Gracie.''

"No, I won't. It's absolutely out of the question. Burt's only been gone for six months. *Six months!* My God, this time last year we were going on vacation.''

She swung out of Gabe's grasp and opened the door. When he tried to take her hand she yanked it out of his reach. "No! This just can't go any further. Do what you and Adeline planned with the comics and let me know if there's anything else you need from me. Otherwise I think it's better if we don't see each other for a while.''

"Gracie—"

"I mean it, Gabe. I mean it," she warned.

And then she ran for home.

Chapter Twelve

It rained for the next three days straight. Gracie thought of it as nature mirroring her feelings—gray and gloomy. By the fourth morning she jumped at an invitation from Dean for dinner.

"I invited myself along," Willy informed her when Gracie arrived at the Mexican restaurant to meet her brother and found her cousin there, too. "I wanted to watch Dean eat crow."

Gracie sat at one of the two empty place settings, across from her brother. "Are you eating crow tonight?" she asked with a confused laugh.

"Afraid so," Dean answered as the waitress set tortilla chips and guacamole in the center of the table, and took their dinner orders.

When she left, Gracie said, "That didn't sound like a crow burrito you ordered, Dean."

"He's been playing detective," Willy offered.

"It just occurred to me the other day that we overlooked one source for confirmation—or lack of it—for your neighbor's claim to the comics," Dean explained.

"That's over and done with," Gracie said.

"I know it is. But I was still worried about the kind of person Duran is, since you were involved with him personally."

"That's over and done with, too." Gracie hated that her voice came out so soft and hurt. She took a chipful of guacamole rather than look at her cousin or brother to see if they'd noticed.

"Well, anyway, I wanted to know," Dean went on. "I persuaded Brandy to ask around and see if she could find out through the grapevine who the group of collectors are. She did and I made a call to some lawyer named Simonesque."

"You didn't say anything to make Gabe look bad, did you?" Gracie asked, alarmed.

Dean rolled his eyes. "No, I didn't. But if you broke up with the guy, why do you care so much?"

"Dragging my feet over selling the comics got him into enough trouble with those collectors. I'd hate for you to have caused him more, is all," she defended herself.

"Okay, okay, so tell her what you found out," Willy prompted.

"Just that there was corroboration for the time span. The date Simonesque gave for when Duran offered the comics was three weeks before Adeline took off—a full two weeks before she knew she'd be leaving for Tibet," Dean said.

"Which means," Willy went on triumphantly, "that Gabe couldn't have had any idea that you were going to inherit the comics or devised some plot to claim them when Adeline wouldn't be around to confirm or refute it because this whole thing started before either of them knew she'd be gone. Adeline had to have been in on the agreement, just the way he said."

"Unless Adeline had refused to sell the comics and he was planning to steal them from her," Dean suggested as if they were brainstorming plot ideas for a TV show.

Gracie and Willy responded to that at the same time, both of them chiding Dean for being ridiculous.

"No matter what Mr. Suspicious here says, you were right to trust Gabe, Gracie," Willy added.

"I didn't doubt it," she said without hesitation, though there was satisfaction in having her trust in him supported and his innocence confirmed.

The waitress came with their meals. When she left Dean said, "Okay, so even I have to admit the guy was on the up-and-up. So, go ahead, Gracie—I know you're dying to say you told me so."

"I was going to ask if this information finally put your mind to rest," Gracie said instead.

"My mind started to rest when you broke up with him."

"Which was the dumbest thing you ever did," Willy said.

"It was not dumb at all, Willy," Dean answered her. "Six months after a death is not enough time to finish grieving and go on to a new man."

"How do you know it isn't? Everybody deals with things in their own way, at their own speed. And Gabe is too good a hunk to let go," Willy countered.

"Thanks for caring, guys," Gracie broke in before Dean could retort again. "But why don't we talk about something else?"

"I just hate that you listened to Dean on this, Gracie. You know how conservative he is when it comes to romance—when it comes to everything," Willy added anyway. "You and Gabe clicked. It's like fate gave you a second guy as good as the first one and you're blowing it."

"I'm just about finished with the tricycle," Gracie said, unsubtly changing the subject.

"At this point in her life she couldn't know if the guy was right for her or not," Dean argued as if Gracie hadn't said a word.

"When it's right, it's right," Willy said.

"And I got a call from the history museum to renovate a chair that dates back to 1770. It's missing a leg, but I think I can make a good match for the other three," Gracie said to the empty fourth seat at the table, exaggerating the fact that her brother and cousin were acting as if she wasn't there.

It didn't matter. Willy and Dean went right on bickering.

"Well, obviously Duran wasn't right for her or she wouldn't have dumped him," Dean said victoriously.

"Then why does she look like that?" Willy demanded, nodding toward Gracie. "She's not sleeping or she wouldn't have those circles under her eyes, and she isn't eating right or her cheeks wouldn't be sinking in again. And—"

"Enough!" Gracie finally cut in, raising her voice loud enough to carry over her cousin's but not so loud that anyone else in the restaurant turned to look. "Would you two knock it off?"

"I just hate for you to lose out on a guy like Gabe," Willy put in petulantly.

"There will be other prospects when the time is right," Dean countered. Then he turned to Gracie. "What were you saying about getting a commission from the history museum?''

Grateful to have at least one of them willing to talk about something else, Gracie launched into that subject. For a few minutes Willy didn't participate at all but after a young, attractive friend of Dean's came to the table to say hello she couldn't resist asking about the man, seeming to forget about Gracie and Gabe's relationship.

From there Gracie managed to keep both her cousin and brother talking about other things through the rest of the meal and all the way out to the parking lot afterward.

But as they said good-night at Gracie's car, Willy started in again. "I'm serious, Gracie. Gabe is too good to turn your back on. Think about what you could have with him, will you?"

Dean clamped his hand around Willy's elbow and pulled her away with him. "Shut up, Wil." Then, over his shoulder, he said, "'Night, Gracie."

Gracie waved and got into her car. Her problem, she thought as she started the engine and pulled out onto the street, was not that she wasn't thinking about Gabe or what she could have had with him. It was that she'd been thinking about it too much. Constantly, in fact. It was hard to live right across the street from him and forget him.

No, that wasn't exactly right. Even if Gabe lived far away she wouldn't have been able to stop thinking about him in the past four days. Their relationship might have been short, but ending it had the power to cause her almost as much pain as Burt's death had.

Somehow the balance of that seemed out of whack, too, she thought. She'd loved Burt for over fifteen years.

How could ending such a brief relationship hurt almost as much?

Maybe because regardless of the length, love was involved in both, she thought. And clearly, time had less significance than the feelings.

She pulled into her driveway—steadfastly refusing to look across the street at Gabe's house—and pushed the button on the remote control that operated the garage-door opener she'd had installed the day before. By the time she drove back to the former carriage house the door was high enough for her to pull in beside the horse tricycle she was nearly finished renovating.

It hadn't been a good choice of projects at this particular time, she'd realized the day after ending things with Gabe. Working on it had brought back too many of her feelings of wanting kids of her own again and thoughts of having them with him.

Was Willy right? she couldn't help asking herself as she walked to the house. Had fate sent her a second chance that she was wasting?

She unlocked the back door and went into the dark, silent house.

"When it's right, it's right," her cousin had said and those words came back to Gracie as she turned on the lights in the kitchen.

What if that was true? Gabe had argued much the same thing—that their relationship had developed so fast and so soon after Burt's death *because* it was right.

It was possible, she conceded.

Gracie did agree with Willy's statement that everyone grieved at a different rate. Her own speed had left her vulnerable and still a little fragile and susceptible to odd moments like the vacation flashback, but for the most part healed. And for all of that she knew she wasn't so vulnerable that just any man could have swept her off her feet the way Gabe had. She'd realized that in the past four days as she'd studied other men—the garage-door installer, actors on TV, guys on the street, in the grocery store, in cars. She wasn't just attracted to anyone with the ability to grow a beard. It was only Gabe she wanted.

But the fact that she'd been widowed for just a short time wasn't the only factor, she reminded herself as she closed the curtains and went to the sink to put the lunch dishes she'd left undone into the dishwasher. There was the length of the relationship itself—mere days. She'd told Gabe that wasn't enough time for them to know each other, and she'd meant it.

And yet as logical as that sounded, she couldn't deny the feeling that she did know him—no matter what she'd claimed when he'd scared her with that marriage proposal.

She knew that he valued family, that he was loyal and committed to his relationships. There was Eli, after all. And even Murf. Another person might not go to the trouble Gabe did to take care of the animal's special needs.

She knew Gabe was kind, thoughtful, compassionate. She'd experienced all of those things herself and seen evidence of them in Adeline's home movies.

She knew he was honest; he hadn't been lying about the comics. And he was patient. He hadn't been pushy even in the face of the pressure of a lawsuit and with so much riding on his need for her to let him sell the magazines.

And he would have accepted her not letting him sell them, Gracie remembered. That was a pretty amazing sign of how much he cared for her, wanted her.

She turned off the water in the sink but she didn't move. Instead, she stood there, staring straight ahead, thinking.

Maybe she shouldn't have let him go.

Gabe was different from Burt, but he had the same values and he was a person she felt she could trust, a person she could count on. That wasn't something easy to find. And like Burt, just the sight of Gabe could chase away any bad feelings she had, could renew her sense of being alive, well, happy. Like Burt, she loved him.

"That's a lot to know about someone," she said.

Should she turn her back on all of that because of the time span? Somehow that suddenly seemed like the least important factor.

The phone rang just then and after the message on her answering machine played, it beeped and Gabe's voice came on.

Gracie froze, unsure whether to pick up or not.

Before she could decide, he'd left a message and the option was gone. And she hadn't even paid attention to what he'd said.

She pushed play, concentrating this time.

The comics were sold and delivered. He had a check for her. He'd like to bring it over. He'd like to talk to her.

His voice sounded tight, tense, sad. But so good, anyway. It washed over her like warm water.

She wanted to see him. She wanted to hear that voice in person. She wanted to touch him, to be touched by him.

She closed her eyes and sighed out a deep breath.

She loved him.

She was sure of it. Sure of him.

Did anything else really matter?

* * *

Murf barked when Gracie rang Gabe's doorbell. It was a deep, booming sound from inside the house that set off a flutter of tension in her stomach.

Remember that Gabe said he wanted to talk, she told herself, feeling as if she might not be welcome here in spite of everything.

He looked surprised to see her when he opened the door. But he recovered quickly and held the screen for her to come in. "Hi."

Gracie pointed a thumb over her shoulder. "I just got your message," she said, wishing her voice hadn't come out sounding so weak and unsure of herself.

She took one step into the house and Murf charged in an unusual burst of energy and jumped up on her, his paws on her shoulders, his rough tongue taking a swipe up her cheek. "Thanks, pal," she said through a grimace.

"Murf!" Gabe reprimanded, pulling him down by the collar. "Sorry. I think the poodle in the yard behind us is in heat and it's made the old boy's hormones perk again."

"You think I remind him of a poodle?"

Gabe laughed spontaneously. "No, he's just full of the devil all of a sudden." Then, as if he'd remembered that things between them weren't all that relaxed, he sobered. "I'd have brought the check over to you."

But it was Gracie who had left him high and dry. It seemed only right that it was Gracie who crossed the street. She just didn't quite know how to get to the reason she was here. "I didn't come for the check."

Gabe struggled to pull Murf to the back door and let him outside. Gracie watched as he did. He obviously hadn't been expecting company because he wore his ratty cutoff shorts and nothing else.

"What did you come for, then?" he asked when he rejoined her in the living room where she waited.

Again she made a nervous gesture to her own house across the street, thinking about his message. "To talk."

He nodded. "Look, I'm sorry about the other night. I didn't mean to scare you."

"It had been a strange day for me. I'd had some flashbacks to last summer when Burt was still alive, and I guess I was a little more raw than I thought."

"Gracie, I—" He reached for her but caught himself and jammed his hands into his back pockets. The action unwittingly served to thrust his bare chest her way and it drew her gaze. As if this were the first time she'd seen it she noticed all over again that it was broad, only slightly spattered with dark hair, that his pectorals were finely developed.

And her hands itched to press his flesh. She imagined that she could feel the heat of him in the centers of her palms. To negate the sensation, she made fists and forced herself to look at his face instead. His oh-so-handsome face, with his rebel good looks and those smoky blue eyes.

She suddenly realized she'd had a lapse of memory— she couldn't recall what they'd been saying—and while she fought for recollection she glanced down at her white jumpsuit and noticed for the first time that Murf had left muddy paw prints down the front of her.

Gabe must have noticed it at the same time because he said, "Look what that damn dog did to you. I'll pay for the cleaning."

"I'll just throw it in the wash," she said, her confidence shaken slightly to realize she'd come here to get him back and now looked like something the dog had literally dragged in. "Anyway," she rushed on, "I wanted to tell you I'm sorry I went a little nuts the other night. That I didn't mean—" She stopped short. What was she going to say? That she didn't mean to turn down his proposal? That's what she'd been thinking. But it wasn't something that could be said. She settled on: "I acted like a nutcase. I'm sorry."

"I want you to know I understand. I rushed you."

"No...I mean, yes, everything happened fast. But after settling down and thinking about it, I realized that you were right...that we're right...together." She was bungling this, she knew. But how did a person gracefully rescind the brutal rejection of a man's proposal?

Then she noticed that Gabe was smiling. "What?" she asked.

"Am I mistaken, or is this an acceptance speech?"

"I never was a very good speaker," she muttered.

"Did you come here tonight to tell me you will marry me, after all?"

"Something like that."

His smile turned into a grin.

But before he said anything else Murf started howling from the yard. "I have to bring him in," Gabe said regretfully, disappearing out the back door.

When he returned he had Murf by the collar again. "You're too old for this," he told the dog as he put him in the garage. Then he turned to Gracie again, smiling. "How about if we do a not-so-instant replay?"

He met her in the center of the living room and pulled her close enough to clasp his hands at the small of her back, his arms draped loosely around her waist. "I'm in love with you, Gracie Canon. I know you've only been a widow for a short time and this probably comes as a surprise to you—especially when we haven't known each other very long—but I don't have a doubt that we're meant for each other and I want you to be my wife.'' That said very formally, he tilted his head to look more closely into her eyes. ''What do you say?''

''Yes?''

''The perfect answer.'' He heaved a sigh of relief, closed his eyes and dropped his forehead to hers. ''This relationship may have happened fast, but the past four days, three hours, sixteen minutes and thirty-eight seconds have been the longest of my life.''

''I haven't been counting, but mine, too.''

He kissed her then, as slowly as if he was savoring something he thought he might never have tasted again.

Gracie let her body melt into his, her hands against his bare back—as hot as she'd imagined before—holding him as he held her.

But a moment later he ended the kiss and clasped her even closer to his chest, his arms enfolding her so tightly she had the sense that he wanted to absorb her into his every pore rather than risk losing her again.

''I love you,'' he said.

''I love you, too. So much.''

His shoulders flexed around her, his head rested atop hers and she could hear his heartbeat under her ear. But she was staring straight at one of his solid-block end tables.

''There is one problem, though,'' she said.

''Nothing that can't be fixed.''

''Do we live in the last century or the next?''

He laughed. ''I think I can live pretty happily in Adeline's house if you think you can make room for a few of my things—the telescope, Murf, the water bed....''

"That big, square box instead of my hand-carved mahogany headboard?" she complained.

"You're a good woman with a saw—can't you rig your headboard to my bed?"

She thought about that. "Maybe," she conceded finally.

"I have faith in your abilities." He stayed holding her for another moment and then said, "I don't want to scare you again, but I want us to get married as soon as possible. Nothing feels right without you."

It made her smile to hear him put into words the sense she'd had in the past four days. "I can't think of any reason for us to wait."

"Tomorrow, then, first thing, we'll get blood tests."

"Okay."

He kissed the top of her head. "That gives us a few hours to fill in the meantime," he said in a raspy, intimate tone.

"Are you telling me that you and Murf have the same thing on your minds?" she teased him.

"Not quite. He just wants to jump that poor poodle's bones. Me, I want to make long, slow love to the muddy woman of my dreams."

"Is there a big distinction between those two?"

"Huge. Let me prove it?"

"Will there be howling involved?"

He squeezed her derriere, drawing her closer still and pulsed his hips against her. "A little moaning, maybe, but no howling."

"Perfect," she answered in a breathy whisper because it was the best she could manage under the wave of desire he was raising in her.

"My place or yours?" he asked.

"Does it matter?"

"Yours has the bathroom for later," he answered in an aside.

"Good point."

"But I'll have to bring my dog."

"It's probably for the best. He'll never get any sleep over here tonight."

Gabe released her and went to get Murf. Then he took Gracie's hand in his free one and led her out into the cool, clear summer night and across the street.

As she approached the old Victorian house Gracie couldn't help smiling and wondering if her aunt would ever know how much she'd really given her.

And then she let Gabe lead her inside where he swept her off her feet and carried her up the stairs to the big feather bed where Gracie had no doubt they'd spend most every night for the rest of their lives.

Thank you, Adeline, she thought just as Gabe came into her arms, her heart full of gratitude to her aunt and love for this man.

*   *   *   *   *

Summer Reading At Its Best

In July, Harlequin and Silhouette bring readers the Big Summer Read Program. Heat up your summer with these four exciting new novels by top Harlequin and Silhouette authors.

SOMEWHERE IN TIME by Barbara Bretton
YESTERDAY COMES TOMORROW by Rebecca Flanders
A DAY IN APRIL by Mary Lynn Baxter
LOVE CHILD by Patricia Coughlin

From time travel to fame and fortune, this program offers something for everyone.

Available at your favorite retail outlet.

BSR